Fledgling

Nicole Conway

Month9Books

Fledgling by Nicole Conway
All rights reserved. Published in the United States of America by Month9Books, LLC.
No part of this book may be used or reproduced in any manner whatsoever without written permission of the publisher, except in the case of brief quotations embodied in critical articles and reviews.

Edited by Georgia McBride
Published by Month9Books
Cover design by Beetiful Book Covers © 2015
Dragon head design by Nicole Conway

Month9Books

To Keith, who first taught me how to fly.

PRAISE FOR FLEDGLING

"Not just another dragon story; this memorable escapade is fast-paced and packed with action. It will leave readers on the edge of their seats" -- D.J. MacHale – Author of "The SYLO Chronicles" and "Pendragon"

"A captivating first installment in an exciting to new series." – Amazon Reviewer

"I would recommend this book for someone who's tired of reading the same old same old. Very inventive and can't wait to see what happens next!" – Amazon Reviewer

"A must read for anyone who loves coming of age stories and dragons!" – Amazon Reviewer

"The book was great. It grabbed my attention from the beginning and held it to the end." – Amazon Reviewer

Fledgling

one

I had never seen my father before my twelfth birthday. Not even once. Up until then, my mother had raised me all by herself in the royal city of Halfax. We lived like all the other gray elves in Maldobar—separated from the rest of society in the heavily guarded wartime ghettos. We had to follow a strict set of rules about where we could go, what we could do, when we got food, and what we could own. If you broke any of the rules, it was an immediate sentence to the prison camps, which I always heard was a fate worse than death. We were supposed to be grateful. After all, we were war refugees. Maldobar didn't have to take us in, much less provide us somewhere to live. This was their act of charity towards us.

Our house was not much more than a tiny shack made of old recycled wood, and it only had one room. You'd expect a place like that to smell terrible, but my mother was a genius when it came to making anywhere feel like home. She could grow absolutely anything, and that was how she made our living. She grew vegetables, flowers, tiny fruit trees, and strange vines that climbed all over the walls and windows. It made the inside of our house feel like a jungle, and it smelled earthy like fresh soil and the fragrance of flowers. We couldn't legally sell anything she grew since gray elves weren't allowed to have any money, but we could still trade. So early in the mornings, my mother packed a sack full of peppers, fruit, vegetables, and anything else ready for harvest, and sent me out to the shops to trade for things we needed.

It was a lot harder than it sounds. Not the trading itself, that part was easy, but I had to be very sneaky about it. I was always on the watch for guards, or humans. Gray elf children were rare, even in the ghettos. Any elf living in the kingdom of Maldobar as a refugee was absolutely not allowed to have children. It was forbidden. Having children was a great way to get thrown into a prison camp, or worse.

But I didn't just have to worry about that. It was bad enough to be a gray elf kid, hiding until you were old enough to be overlooked. But I was a halfbreed. My father was a human from Maldobar. So instead of looking at me with anger, everyone looked at me like I was a cockroach. The humans didn't like me touching their stuff because I was mixed with the filthy, wild blood of a gray elf. If they hadn't liked my mother's produce so much, they probably would have turned me in to the guards. The gray elves didn't like me, either. But there was a very strict code amongst them: you didn't betray your own kind no matter what. So they ignored me rather than ratting me out to the city guards.

I really didn't fit anywhere, except with my mother. She loved me unconditionally. She was the most beautiful person in the world. Her hair was long and silvery white, and her eyes were like stars. All gray elves had eyes like that. When she smiled at me, her eyes would shine like gemstones in the light, as white and pale as diamonds with faint flecks of blue, yellow, and green in them.

When she died, I had just turned twelve. I got the feeling right away that no one really knew what to do with me. I didn't fit into anyone's plans. If I were a pure blooded elf, they would have taken me straight to a prison camp. If I were a human, someone would have adopted me. I wasn't either, and yet I was both at the same time. I think the guards were just baffled that my mother had done such a good job of hiding me for so long, or that she'd somehow managed to have an affair with a human man.

Ulric Broadfeather was the only one who would take me in, and I'm pretty sure he only did it because my mother had left a letter behind naming him as my biological father. If it weren't for the public shame of disowning a child, he probably would have just let me go to a prison camp anyway.

From the very beginning, my father was the most frightening man I had ever known. He was hugely tall, like a knight, and stronger than anyone else I had ever seen. Once, I saw him pick up and pull the family wagon while it was loaded with bags of grain all by himself. He could have crushed my neck with one hand if he wanted to. His hair was jet-black like mine, except it was cut short. My mom always insisted I wear my hair long, like gray elves traditionally did. I also had his cold blue eyes that were the same color as glacier water. There definitely wasn't any doubt he was my father. I looked too much like him for anyone to deny it.

I wish I could say that he welcomed me with open arms into his home; eager to make up for lost time he hadn't gotten to spend with me. But he already had a family, living on the outskirts of a small city called Mithangol, and he wasn't interested in adding me to it. I was an unwanted guest right away.

He had a human wife named Serah who made it perfectly clear she didn't want me in her house at all. Serah absolutely hated me. She glared whenever she looked at me, accused me of being responsible for anything that went wrong, and refused to let me sleep in her house because I gave her a "bad feeling."

So I slept on a cot in the loftroom of Ulric's workshop, instead. As bad as it sounds, I actually preferred it. It was quiet there, and even though it was cold in the winter, I liked the smell of the old hay and the leather that was stored up there.

Ulric also had another son, Roland, who was four years older than me. Roland chose to ignore my existence completely. I got the feeling that he was in survival mode, trying to be as aloof and uninvolved with the family as he possibly could until he was old enough to move out. I couldn't really blame him for that. Like me, he favored our father. He was really tall, muscular, and had the same ice-blue eyes that looked like they belonged to a powerful bird of prey. I was a little afraid of him, even though he never said more than two words to me at a time. I could sense a lot of anger coming from him, and I was always paranoid I'd be standing too close when he finally snapped.

Ulric had two more children, a pair of twin daughters named Emry and Lin. They were six years younger than me, but they were meaner than a pair of hungry jackals. Every day, they tried to get me in as much trouble as possible. Of course, Serah believed every word they said. They would break things, let the chickens and goats out, or steal jewelry from their mother's room, and blame it all on me. Once, Emry got ahold of the sewing scissors and chopped up Lin's hair. When Serah found out, Emry blamed it all on me and told her I had done it. Serah believed it, and I got a beating from Ulric as soon as he came in the house. Inventing new ways to get me into trouble was their favorite pastime, and there was nothing I could do about it. They were sneaky and smart, a lot smarter than me I guess, because they never got caught.

The only good thing about living with my father was watching him work. Ulric was a tackmaster—he made saddles for the dragonriders from Blybrig Academy. But he didn't just make saddles; he made the very best saddles in Maldobar. I watched him through the slats and gaps in the floor of the loftroom, shaping leather and stitching intricate pieces together. He did it all by hand, and it took him several weeks to craft one saddle. But when it was finished, each one was the most beautiful thing I'd ever seen. It made me envy him, even if he probably wished I had never been born.

That's why I almost keeled over when Ulric growled my name, calling me down from my room into his shop. He'd been working for two weeks solid on a new saddle, one more beautiful than ever, and it was finally finished.

"Wrap it up," he barked at me in his gruff, gravely tone, and threw a few old quilts at me.

I was stunned. Ulric had never asked me to do anything before, especially nothing to do with his work. This was my chance, I thought. If I could be useful, maybe he wouldn't hate me so much. He might even teach me to make saddles someday.

Ulric left me alone in his shop, and I walked over to the saddle that was set up on one of the big sawhorses. I ran my fingers over the freshly oiled leather. It was as red as blood, engraved with intricate designs and images of mountains and vines. All the buckles were made of silver-plated iron. I couldn't even imagine what it would look like when the dragon it had been made for would finally put it on. A powerful beast, bound for the skies with a snarl and a flash of fire. It made my skin prickle, and every hair stand on end.

I was small for my age. Ulric's stature apparently hadn't been passed on to me. To make matters worse, I was so skinny that I pretty much looked like a scarecrow. Emry and Lin like to call me "stick boy" because they knew it bothered me. If I were as big as Roland, no one would have tried to push me around.

It took all my strength to wrap the saddle up in the quilts so it wouldn't get scratched or damaged, and then lug it outside. The weight of it made my arms and lungs ache. I could feel myself wobble dangerously if I leaned too far in any direction. I didn't want to imagine what Ulric would do to me if I dropped this saddle.

The knights who rode on dragons just about never came to pick up their saddles personally. Most of them came from rich, powerful noble families, and had plenty of servants to do those kinds of errands for them. So when I saw Ulric standing outside talking to a man in formal battle armor with a sweeping cape of royal blue brushing at his heels, I stopped dead in my tracks. The saddle weighed more than I did, and I almost dropped it in surprise.

It was a muggy, overcast day. The clouds were so low and thick you couldn't see the mountains that hunched over our small city. Even so, the knight's armor still managed to gleam like liquid silver. He had his helmet under one arm, the white-feathered crest on it tipped in black, and the king's eagle engraved upon his breastplate.

They both turned to look at me as I stood there, my arms shaking under the weight of the saddle, staring at the dragonrider. Ulric scowled darkly, and stomped over to take it from me. He slung it over his shoulder like it weighed nothing at all, growling curses under his breath at me as he went to tie it down to the knight's horse.

The knight, however, was still staring right at me. He gave me a strange look, narrowing his eyes some and tilting his head to the side slightly like he was sizing me up. It made me blush from head to toe, the tips of my pointed ears burning like torches under my long hair. This was a warrior who had probably fought against gray elves for years, and I knew what I looked like.

He curled a finger at me, calling me toward him. It made me cringe as I obeyed. I hedged toward him, my shoulders hunched up because I half-expected him to hit me just out of pure resentment for what I was. But he didn't.

When I got close enough, he grabbed my chin in one of his gloved hands, cranking my head around so I had to look up at him. I was shaking all over, wondering if this was it for me. Maybe he'd crush my head like a grape in his hand. Or maybe he'd throttle me to death. Either way, I was pretty sure Ulric wouldn't go out of his way to save me. He might have even thanked the knight afterwards for saving him the trouble.

"What's your name, boy?" The knight asked me. His voice was deep, but not angry or resentful. He was turning my head this way and that, pulling back my hair to see my pointed ears, and looking me over like he was inspecting livestock.

"J-Jaevid." I told him through clattering teeth.

He frowned, looking back into my eyes before he finally let me go. His own eyes seemed dead to me.

Dead—like someone who had seen many years in battle and knew what it meant to kill without mercy.

"How old are you?" he asked again.

"Fifteen, sir." I took a few steps back away from him. If he came after me suddenly, at least I had some hope of outrunning him. I was small, but I was fast.

Ulric was finished tying the saddle down, and came over with a growl meant to shoo me away. I took the hint and retreated back into the workshop, up to my loftroom where I had a wooden cot piled with old, holey quilts. I went to the small window along the far wall. It was a good place to peek at them through the cracks in the boards that had been nailed over it. I could hear them talking, and it made my heart jump into my throat.

"You didn't tell me you had a halfbreed son," the knight chuckled, like it was a bad joke. "Looks just like a half-starved, miniature version of you, except for the ears."

Ulric just shook his head and kept growling rumbling words, glaring at the ground. "Serah wants him gone." I heard him say.

"Can't blame her for that." The knight seemed to sympathize. "You thinking of taking him on as an apprentice?"

Ulric just snorted like it was a ridiculous idea.

"Ah, my mistake then. I figured since your older

boy had chosen to join the infantry you'd pass your skill set onto someone else in your family. I doubt your girls would be interested." The knight rambled on, beginning to stroll back to where his horse was waiting. The new saddle was bundled up and ready for transport. "A shame he's such a small, sickly-looking thing."

That stung me. Yes, I was small for my age. But I hadn't thought I looked sickly. It made me angry at myself, and at my inability to grow even a few inches taller. What a difference even two inches and a few pounds of muscle would have made.

"Where's his dragon?" A whispering voice suddenly asked from right beside me.

It scared me out of my wits, making me scramble away. I was half afraid it was one of my sisters. But it wasn't.

Katalina Crookin was probably the only friend I had in the world. Her father was a very good blacksmith who worked with Ulric sometimes, helping him craft unique pieces that required a more skilled metalworker. They only lived about a mile away, so Katty and I had found each other inevitably. She was small and skinny, like I was, with a head full of wild gold curls. She had big dark blue eyes, and just about every inch of her face was covered in freckles. The other kids in town teased her and called her ugly. I knew it must have hurt her feelings, but she never let it show. And when the other kids would come after me, trying to cut my hair or throw rocks at me, she was always there to defend me ... and no one could throw a rock harder or more accurately than Katty. She had blacksmith's hands.

I shook my head at her, moving back to the window to peek outside again. The knight was getting on his horse already, dropping a purse of coins into Ulric's hand before he rode out of sight.

"I don't know. I don't think he brought it," I whispered back. Neither of us had ever seen a dragon before.

Katty puffed a sigh of disappointment while shaking her head. It made her gold curls swish back and forth. "I saw him coming up the road. I knew he had to be a dragonrider. Normal soldiers don't wear armor like *that*," she told me. "Can you come over today?"

I didn't know. Normally, I could've easily slipped away to visit the Crookins without Ulric or Serah even noticing I was gone because usually, they didn't care where I was. But Ulric had actually asked me to do something for him today. Not to mention, he and the knight had been discussing my future—or lack thereof. I wasn't so sure I could get away with leaving without getting caught.

Katty was watching me waffle between my desire to go to her house, and the inevitable beating I would get if

Ulric ever caught me over there. She smiled. "Momma's making sweetbread," she baited me. "With wild honey."

That decided it for me. I grinned back at her, nodding because we both knew what goodies were sure to go along with sweetbread. Thoughts of whipped butter with cinnamon and sugar, and warm milk with a hint of honey, were already swimming happily through my brain as we climbed down from my loftroom. We darted out the back of Ulric's shop before anyone noticed, and took the narrow footpath we'd made ourselves through the prickly briars. It was our secret path, so no one would see us.

The Crookin's house was not as big as ours, but it felt more like a home instead of the prison I lived in. Smoke came out of the chimney in the house, and out of the stack for the bellows in Mr. Crookin's forge. Mr. Crookin didn't really like me. That's not to say he hated me as much as Serah did, but he didn't like me coming around his house too often. He hadn't minded it so much when I was younger, but now that I was fifteen, I could tell he was on the verge of telling me not to come back anymore. He didn't talk much, and he had a face that was mostly hidden behind a thick, wiry beard. He wore his long black smithing apron every day, and his face and arms were almost always smeared with soot.

Mrs. Crookin, on the other hand, was one of the few

people who didn't make me feel unwanted. She smiled at me when we came inside, wiping her hands on her apron before she pulled me in immediately to kiss my forehead and ruffle my hair. She always hugged me until I couldn't breathe, and asked me if I was getting enough to eat.

"What a good boy," she said, patting my cheeks until it stung a little. "But still so skinny. Doesn't Serah feed you at all? Sit down, Jae. I'm making your favorite."

Katty plopped down in a chair across from me at their kitchen table, grinning as she slid a plate and spoon in my direction. "There was a dragonrider at his house today, momma." Her eyes were still sparkling with excitement about it.

"Yeah, but he didn't bring his dragon." I added, sighing and twirling the spoon through my fingers.

Mrs. Crookin brought over a platter of steaming hot sweetbread, fresh out of the oven. The smell made me dizzy with hunger, and it was hard to sit and wait while she put out jams, that delicious cinnamon butter, and mugs of warm milk for us on the table. "Not surprising, is it dear? It's nearly springtime."

I knew what she meant. Every spring, Ulric packed up his tools and materials onto a wagon, and left for Blybrig Academy. The new riders started their training just as the weather was getting hot, and Ulric had to take molds and build brand new saddles for them. It was when he made most of his money, but it also meant that he'd be gone for a while. He was always completely exhausted when he came back. In a month, the snows would melt in the Stonegap Pass, and Ulric would start packing his tools again. If any other knights wanted a saddle from him, they'd have to get it before he left, or wait until after spring.

"I wish papa would let me go with him," Katty whined while she was smearing a spoonful of jam onto a large piece of bread. "It's not fair. Other apprentices get to go."

"Soon, dear." Mrs. Crookin smiled fondly at her daughter. They had the same gold colored hair, but Mrs. Crookin's was flecked with silver. She was a much older woman than my stepmother.

Katty was eager to go to Blybrig, not that I could blame her. She wanted to see dragons just like I did. Her father had been teaching her his craft for a long time, and she was already strong enough to do most of the little tedious jobs for him, even if she was small and fragile looking. Mr. Crookin went to Blybrig for spring training, just like Ulric. But he went to make armor, not saddles.

"You'll have to tell me what they look like," I told her. I wasn't able to keep myself from sounding sad about it. When she starting working with her father full time, I wasn't sure where that would leave me. I'd be on the brink of adulthood with no idea where I should go, or what I should do. I wouldn't have a skill to sell, or even a place to live.

Katty smiled at me hopefully from across the table, leaning forward and grabbing my hand at the wrist. "You'll see them, too, Jae. Maybe papa would let you be his apprentice with me."

Mrs. Crookin smiled at us, but I could still see it in her eyes; she didn't think her husband would ever allow that. They were all right with me coming to visit, and with me being friends with their daughter, but they had to draw the line somewhere. I was still a halfbreed.

I didn't let Katty see how that hurt me. It wasn't their fault, really. And it wasn't my place to try to weasel my way into their family business like that. "Nah." I shrugged and gave her as confident a grin as I could muster. "I'm going to the coast. I want to work on one of the ships going out of the harbor. I'll get to see the ocean, and eat fish every night."

Katty looked deflated. I guess she'd wanted us to work together. Or, she'd at least hoped I would want the same thing as her. "You'll smell like a fish, after all that," she grumbled, wrinkling her nose.

We ate until there were only a few scraps of the bread left, and Mrs. Crookin wrapped those up for me to take. It was dark outside when I started for home. Katty always walked with me as far as the property line, and she had a blanket wrapped around her so that only her face and some of her curls peeked out.

"Jae," she started. I could tell by the tone of her voice she was about to ask me something serious. "Do you really want to go to the coast?"

I've never been a very good liar. When it came to Katty, well, she could smell deception on me like a hound. I couldn't lie to her if I wanted to. I quirked my mouth while I thought about the ocean, about ships, and about eating fish.

"Not really," I confessed.

"We'd never see each other if you left," she reached a hand out from under her blanket to grasp mine, squeezing my fingers. "After papa retires and I take over the business, I'll make you an apprentice myself. Then we can work together and no one will be able to say anything about it."

I tried to smile for her. I tried to show her some optimism. But we'd be in our twenties before her father let her take on any authority in his smithing business, and even then, I wasn't sure blacksmithing was my calling. It required physical strength, which I clearly didn't have.

"Thanks, Katty." I squeezed her hand back.

We talked about dragons and knights all the way to the property line. Then I gave her a hug, and she kissed my cheek like her mom did, and we parted ways. I walked a few feet into the dark before I stopped and looked back, watching her disappear into the gloom and thorny shrubs. She was the best friend I had—my only friend really, and sooner or later, she'd have to leave me behind. She'd outgrow me. She'd get tired of having to stick up for me all the time.

With the bundle of leftover bread still under my arm, I walked back to my room in the loft. Ulric's shop was quiet and dark, like it always was once he'd finished for the day. He was probably already inside, having dinner with his real family, and talking about how soon he could get rid of me. Roland was probably just sitting there at the table, glaring down into his plate without a word. The twins were probably throwing food at each other like savages. I didn't expect any of them to even notice I was gone.

But I was wrong.

two

Ulric was waiting for me in the dark. I didn't see him until I had already shut the shop door and turned around to go up the rickety ladder to the loft. I smacked right into him, bouncing off his chest like a rubber ball, and landing squarely on my rump at his feet. I dropped the package of bread scraps, and they scattered out all over the ground.

"Where have you been?" Ulric's voice boomed in the dark like thunder.

Before I could even think about answering, much less running, he had me by the hair. He yanked me to my feet and pushed me up against the wall, kicking the scraps of bread across the floor all the while.

"Stealing from the neighbors?" He reared back a hand to smack me across the face so hard it felt like my eyeballs might pop out of their sockets. "Or squeezing on their daughter?"

I hadn't been stealing or squeezing, but I knew better than to try to tell him that. My cheek was burning like it was on fire when he smacked me again on the other side of my face even harder. As much as I tried not to cry, I couldn't keep my eyes from watering up. I was terrified of him already, and now I was afraid he might just solve his own problem and kill me. No one would ask questions about where I had gone, except for maybe Katty and her mother.

"If I ever catch you running off this property again, I'll beat your skull inside out," he promised, yanking me away from the wall and flinging me toward the ladder. I hit it before I could catch myself. My head cracked off edge of the ladder, making me see bright spots of light in my vision.

"Get up there," he snarled at my back. It made a cold pang of fear shoot through me like a lightning bolt. "And you better have yourself down here ready to work as soon as the sun is up tomorrow. Understood?"

I scrambled up the ladder with my ears ringing and my vision swerving. I didn't stop to ask any questions. I didn't even realize what he'd said until I was curled up underneath my cot, shaking with fear, and anticipating hearing Ulric scaling the ladder to come after me. Instead, I heard the shop door slam, lock, and the crunch of his footsteps storming back toward the house.

I was bewildered. It wasn't the first time Ulric had come after me swinging, but he'd caught me completely off guard this time. My heart was still drumming in my ears when I finally dared to crawl out from under my bed. I touched my cheeks, wincing at how they still stung. I probably had handprints on both sides of my face.

Ulric had never wanted me anywhere near his work until today. Now he was ordering me to help him? I couldn't even begin to guess why, and it made my head spin with the possibilities and hopes that seemed too stupid to say out loud. I wanted to believe that maybe, just maybe, he was going to let me be his apprentice. If he taught me his trade—heck, if he taught me anything at all—I was prepared to learn as much as I could. I needed this if I was ever going to get out from under his roof.

I didn't sleep at all. I lay awake until the sun started to rise, thinking about what I'd be in for the next day, and whether or not I would able to do whatever Ulric asked of me. Being willing was one thing, but being physically capable was another. My heart could be in it all day long, but I couldn't will myself into greater strength.

When I heard Ulric unlocking his shop, I was on my

feet and in my shoes, waiting for him down the ladder before he could even swing the door open. He glared down at me like he'd found a dead mouse in his shoe, brushing past me without a word.

I stood awkwardly by the door with my hands clenched into fists, and my feet ready to run in case he turned on me again. He started into a routine I knew all too well. I'd seen him pack up his tools before, and it made my stomach twist into those painful, hopeful knots all over again.

"Sweep out the mess you made," he mumbled with his back to me. "Then hitch up the wagon, and bring it around."

"Yes sir," I answered quickly, and went to get the broom. I swept away the dried up leftovers of Mrs. Crookin's bread that were still scattered on the floor. I swept the whole shop out, working so quickly that it had me sweating before I went outside into the cold morning air.

The fog was still thick and heavy, making the steep countryside look ominous and grim as I went to the barn and brought out the old draft horse Ulric used to pull his wagon. The giant horse could've kicked my head off if he'd had the mind to, but the sad old thing didn't act like he had enough energy to trot, much less kick anyone. I hitched him to the small cart Ulric used every spring to carry his tools and materials to Blybrig.

When I led the horse and wagon around to the workshop, Ulric was already stacking crates outside to load onto it. He commanded me to help him, and I tried my best. My arms weren't strong enough to lift the heavy wooden crates full of tools, but I could carry the sawhorses, and I helped pile the rolls of uncut leather onto the wagon. We covered everything with blankets to offer some protection from the elements, and tied ropes tautly over the load to keep anything from falling out during the trip.

By that time my clothes and hair were absolutely drenched with sweat. I stood back, not looking for any gratitude from my father, but hoping for at least some acknowledgement that I'd done a good job. He didn't even look at me on his way to climb up into the driving seat of the wagon, grumbling under his breath the whole way.

Serah came out of the house carrying a big bag I knew would be packed with plenty of food and changes of clothes to last him the journey. I knew better than to think there'd be anything for me in that bag. She handed it up to him, and the two just exchanged a stiff, stern-faced stare before she backed away and crossed her arms. Her cold eyes flicked to me, her face looking sharper and angrier than usual. Sometimes I got the feeling she blamed me for my own existence, or that she was jealous of any attention Ulric gave me that didn't involve punishing me for something.

"Just going to stand there like an idiot?" Ulric barked at me suddenly.

My mouth opened, and no sound came out. I didn't know what to say, or what he expected me to do.

He jerked his head, gesturing to the driver's seat beside him.

My heart jumped. I still couldn't move, much less speak. I was terrified of making the mistake of assuming he actually wanted me to go with him. I took a few steps, and Serah's venomous glare stopped me dead in my tracks.

"Get over here, you dumb kid." Ulric growled in a dangerous tone. "You're wasting daylight."

It was a leap of faith, to think I was invited on this trip. But I took it. I walked quickly past Serah with my head bowed low, avoiding meeting her eyes, and climbed up to sit on the driver's seat beside my father. He didn't wait until I was settled or even balanced to snap the reins. The wagon lurched into motion, and I almost fell over the seat.

We took off at as fast a trot as the old horse could manage, leaving Serah and the house in a swirling cloud of dust behind us. It started to sink in, then. I was going to Blybrig Academy. I was going to learn to make dragon saddles. Either that, or Ulric was going to drop me off at a prison camp on the way there.

My father waited until we were out of sight of the house to pull a wad of chewing tobacco from his pocket and cram it into his mouth. Serah hated it when he chewed that stuff, and even more when he spit it into her gardens. He didn't say a word to me as we rattled down the road, and I couldn't think of a good reason to try to talk to him, either.

When we passed the Crookin's house, I leaned to look up the twisting dirt path that led to their house. I craned my neck, hoping to catch a glimpse of Katty helping her mother hang laundry, or feeding their chickens, so I could wave goodbye to her. She'd know just as soon as she saw me sitting in the wagon with my father that I was going to Blybrig. She'd be so happy, knowing we'd see each other there eventually. But I didn't see her or her mother, and it made me slump back into my seat with disappointment. Maybe she'd figure it out, or maybe I could write her a letter once I got to Blybrig.

It took a long, exhausting, miserable week to get from Mithangol to Blybrig Academy. The only thing worse than being at home with my father was being alone with him. We didn't talk. He didn't say anything to me at all. There was always tension in the air, and it made it hard for me to feel safe. I was afraid to turn my back to him while we were out here, alone in the wild.

The road wound away from our little city, twisting through the high cliffs, and carving a steep path upwards through the Stonegap Mountains. The higher we went, the thinner the air got. It got dryer, too, and made my throat feel raw. My lips were chapped and peeling, but Ulric wouldn't let me have any more than the small ration of water he'd planned out for us every day.

At night, we ate a little bit of dinner that consisted of flatbread and some dried meat, and then went straight to bed. Ulric had a bedroll, and he slept by the fire on the ground. I curled up with a blanket on the seat of the wagon, looking up at the stars in the cold night sky. Some nights, it was too cold to sleep at all, and I sat up by the fire on the ground, my teeth chattering and my toes numb, until morning.

That's when I thought about my mom. When I was alone like that at night, when it was quiet, I always thought about her. I took out the necklace she'd given me when I was little. I kept it hidden under my tunic. I didn't want anyone to see it, and no one except for Katty even knew that I had it. It was carved from white bone, engraved with designs and words in elven that I didn't understand. It hung around my neck on an old leather cord, exactly where she'd put it the day she gave it to me. I rubbed it with my fingers while I remembered my mom. The memories I had of her voice, her face, and her smell were all beginning to fade. I was afraid that eventually I'd forget her completely.

I felt like I'd been dragged behind the wagon, rather than riding in it, all week when we finally reached Blybrig. I was tired, sore, hungry, and thirsty. Even Ulric was beginning to look pretty road-weary and miserable. We didn't have much left in the way of supplies, and I was beginning to worry we might run out before we got to the academy.

Then all of a sudden, none of that mattered. As we crested one final, steep rise in the road through Stonegap Pass, I got my first look down into the valley hidden below.

They called it the Devil's Cup because the land in the valley was so arid and dry. It was a small desert nestled into a crescent of mountains, cut off from the rest of the world except for Stonegap Pass—unless you could fly. The only small portion of the valley that wasn't guarded by white-peaked mountains bordered the coastline and looked out to nothing but blue ocean. I could see the water, sparkling in the distance, and stretching out across the horizon beyond.

I saw it all, spread out before me so suddenly that it took my breath away. I couldn't help but stand up to get a better look, able to see exactly how the road wound down the mountainside into the valley. It twisted across the parched earth, past thorny shrubs and cacti, until it stopped before the only standing structure in the whole valley: Blybrig Academy.

Then I saw them. What I'd mistaken for a flock of birds circling far overhead weren't birds at all. The nearer they came, the more aware I became of their size. They were huge, bigger than any animal I'd ever seen, with powerful wings stretched to the morning sun. Dragons were everywhere I looked, flying in V-shaped formations overhead in groups of two or more. The light danced off the gleaming armor of the knights riding on their backs. They soared like eagles, majestic and graceful, riding the wind that blew in from the ocean. They were perched on the high circular ramparts that enclosed the academy complex, and even from a distance, I could hear their bellowing calls.

We rattled down the road that led up to the only gate in and out of Blybrig. The walls were enormous, at least five stories tall, and made of stacked grey stones that looked like they had been mined right out of the mountains surrounding the valley. The enormous iron gates stood wide open, letting us into the world of the dragonriders—a place only a select few actually got to see.

As I understood it, its location was secret. Only

dragonriders and the craftsmen who worked for them actually knew where this place was. That had seemed ridiculous to me before, but now that I'd been through that grueling, narrow, and dangerous path that was the only way through the mountains, I understood. If you didn't already know where this place was, odds were you weren't going to find it just wandering by around in the mountains.

Ulric drove the wagon through the gate and into the complex, passing students and knights on the way. All the buildings seemed to be set up around one central, massive circular structure. It had a covered domed roof, and the entire thing looked like one large cave carved right out of the rock.

"The breaking dome," Ulric explained when he saw me staring at it. I was surprised he'd actually cared enough about my interest to say anything at all, but maybe this was part of the job. I needed to know where everything was so I could run errands for him.

"What's it for?" I dared to try my luck to see how much he was willing to tell me.

Ulric just shrugged and made a grunting sound at first, leaning to spit some of his tobacco juice onto the ground. He'd been chewing it nearly nonstop since we'd left home. "Training."

I stared at the massive structure as we passed it. It was

hard not to feel intimidated by it. It looked like a giant stone turtle shell, with a rounded opening like a gaping maw. As our wagon rolled by it, I was almost certain I heard it growl.

Ulric pointed out the buildings the further we went into the complex. There were two dormitories, one meant for instructors and high-ranking riders, and another for students. They both looked the same on the outside, the same height and shape, with narrow windows. There was a separate place for academics, and a gymnasium for combat training.

One very long, especially strange-looking building was set at the back, directly behind the central dome. It looked like a dollhouse with one wall missing so that you could see all the rooms inside it. Extending from each of the ten levels were platforms made from iron beams laid out like latticework. I watched the dragons come in close to the building, flaring their wings to slow their speed, and stretching out their strong back legs to grip the platform with curled talons as they landed. It was like a stable for dragons, with each room being a separate stall for a dragon to nest in. Ulric said they called it the Roost.

We stopped at last outside of one of the two armory houses. One was set up especially for blacksmiths, with already established forges and plenty of room for the smiths to work fashioning and repairing armor. Its tall chimneys belched black smoke into the air, and I could smell the familiar scent of scorched metal. It reminded me of Katty's house.

As soon as we found our workstation in the armory house meant for tackmasters, Ulric backed the wagon up to it, and we started to unload all the crates and rolls of leather. He put me to work opening the crates with a pry bar, telling me to set out his tools while he went to stable the horse.

Even here, in the desert valley of Devil's Cup, it was still cool this early in the spring. But the air was so dry, and I was so tired already, it didn't take me ten minutes to be drenched with sweat again. I tied my hair back to get it away from my face, not thinking about it until I heard someone say the word "*halfbreed.*"

Then I remembered. Tying my hair back like that exposed my pointed ears. They weren't elongated and slender like a full blooded gray elf's would have been, but their subtle points were definitely noticeable. And people were definitely beginning to notice.

There was a group of four older boys standing just outside Ulric's workstation, and they were staring right at me. I didn't know any of them, but I could tell they were new students right away. They weren't wearing uniforms or armor yet, and they all looked seventeen. Naturally, they were all a good foot taller than I was, and I knew they were laughing at me even without looking up to make sure.

I tried to ignore them. Nothing good would happen if I said anything back, and I didn't have much of an ego left to defend anyway. They could say what they wanted; I'd come here to work.

I was stacking the empty crates outside our workstation, making room for dragons to be brought inside like Ulric had told me to, when I felt someone pull my hair. Someone grabbed my ponytail, and yanked it hard enough to make me fall backwards. The empty crate landed squarely on my chest.

It knocked the breath right out of me, and I laid there for a few seconds looking up into the sky and the glare of the sun in a daze. I thought maybe I'd imagined it. Maybe I'd just tripped. But then a menacing face appeared over me. One of the guys who had been laughing at me earlier was leaning over, smirking and looking back to his friends for approval. For some reason bullies always needed validation that they were doing a good job. Or at least, it seemed that way to me.

"What are you doing here, scum?" He sneered down at me. "We don't like traitors, you know." I watched him disappear, and then a few seconds later, there was a boot in my face. He put the heel of his shoe on my forehead and started to grind it back and forth.

I hadn't even thought about fighting back yet. I was just trying to figure out how to get the boot off my face and the crate off my chest. But suddenly both were gone, and I heard the group of older boys cursing and yelling.

Rolling over to cough and blink the dirt out of my eyes, I lifted my head to see a much larger, fully armored man holding the boy who'd been using me as his doormat by the ear. The knight was pinching the boy's ear in his gauntlet-covered hand, making him scream in pain, before finally letting him go. Something about the knight was familiar. I couldn't figure out what it was until he was standing over me, grabbing me by the arm and hauling me back to my feet.

"You attract a lot of attention, boy." The knight's voice was immediately familiar. It was the same one who had come to pick up his saddle from our house.

I opened my mouth to say something, and immediately forgot what it was. I hadn't expected anyone to come to my rescue, least of all a knight. I remembered to at least be grateful. "Thank you, sir."

He made an annoyed sound as he removed his white-crested helmet. Now I was certain it was the same knight from before. He looked down at me with his sea green eyes narrowed and scrutinizing. His dark hair was cut very short and beginning to turn gray around his temples. Even though his skin was weathered, there was still something wild and unpredictable in his eyes, which made it hard to place his age. Still, I couldn't imagine him being any older than Ulric.

"You should keep a low profile," he warned me. "Unless you intend on growing a spine in the near future."

Couldn't he see me? Sure, standing up to bullies and the other kids who gave me a hard time sounded good in theory, but I knew better. I had no chance of ever winning a fight like that. Better to let them kick me around some, use me as a doormat, and get away with no broken bones, than get my arms cracked off just to prove a point.

"Save it, Sile. The kid's a coward. Better that way. He'll live longer if he keeps his mouth shut." Ulric's voice growled, surprising me as he strolled up behind us. Immediately, I went back to work moving crates.

The knight frowned at me, looking disappointed, and I tried not to notice. It made an urgent feeling twist in the pit of my stomach, so I turned my back to him while I worked and tried not to listen to anything else they said.

"Who is that?" I asked when the knight finally left to go back about his business.

Ulric was setting up sawhorses, and scowling at all the work I'd done like none of it was up to his standard. But I never saw him fix anything. He made another annoyed grunting sound in response to my question.

"Sile Derrick," he answered, and spat another mouthful of putrid tobacco juice on the ground. "Stay away from him. He should mind his own business, instead of telling me how to mind mine."

We got the workshop ready just after sundown. It took a long time for me to drag out base molds and fill them with packed wax shavings from huge sacks I had to drag out of a storeroom. My arms were sore, and my stomach was growling so loudly I knew everyone could hear it. I'd never been so tired in all my life, but when Ulric glanced at me, I tried to look as composed and ready to work as I'd ever been.

"We start at dawn," he told me, finally spitting out the wad of tobacco he'd been gnawing on into a trash barrel. "You sleep in here, and mind our stuff. Have the molds ready when I get here."

Ulric left me standing in the workshop, wondering what I was supposed to eat or where I could sleep, as he disappeared into the complex. I was immediately afraid. After the sun had set, the air had gotten very cold, and the wind howled through the valley making an eerie, screaming sound.

I couldn't find anything to eat, but there were a few good swallows of water left in one of the canteens we'd used on our journey here. I found Ulric's sleeping pallet and unrolled it in a corner of the shop behind a few stacked up crates of materials where no one would be able to see me. I didn't want to run the risk of those older boys finding me again.

Hours passed. It was bitter cold. Even under the two quilts I had, I was still freezing. More than anything, though, I was starving. I hadn't had a good meal since Mrs. Crookin's bread, and thoughts of those wasted crumbs were making my stomach tie up in knots. It hurt so much it put tears in my eyes. I didn't know how I was going to find the strength to work the next day if I didn't get something to eat before then.

Sometime after midnight, I just couldn't take it anymore. I got to my feet in pitch black, and snuck out of the workshop. The complex was quiet in the dead of night. Almost all the students and riders were asleep, and their dragons were snug in the Roost. Only a few were still out flying low patrol patterns around the walls. I couldn't see them, but I could hear the hum of the wind off their wings and long scaled tales whenever they swooped in close.

I was looking for anything edible I could get my hands on without being caught. I walked past the two armories, spotting the smoldering fires from the forge that still glowed. I wondered if I could sneak in there to sleep. At least it would be warmer closer to the forge.

On my way past the breaking dome, my steps got

slower, until finally I was standing before the gaping doorway, staring into it with my skin shivering. It felt deep and monstrously dark in there, as though it were the bottomless abyss of some dark cave.

That's when I heard it. Before, I thought I was only imagining that building growling at me. This time I was sure.

A deep, rumbling growl echoed from within, and I tripped over my feet backing away from it. I looked back over my shoulder. There was no one else there. No one was watching, or playing some kind of trick on me. But I didn't feel like I was alone. There was definitely something in that deep, dark cavern of a building, and it felt like it was calling out to me.

three

I knew I should have just gone back to the workstation and tried sleeping again. Ulric might remember to bring me something to eat in the morning, if I was lucky. After all, nothing good could possibly come from nosing around in the secret places of the academy. Going into the breaking dome alone so late at night was a terrible idea. Probably the worst idea I'd had yet.

I had almost talked myself out of it. I was scared of what I'd find in there, or worse, of getting caught red-handed by my father. Whenever I got caught somewhere I wasn't supposed to be, people tended to suspect the worst right away. I'd probably get accused of being a traitor again, or a spy, or something ridiculous like that.

If the gray elves were going to try to spy on Blybrig, I was pretty sure I'd be the last person in the world they'd ever want to send to do it. Too bad no one else was ever going to agree with me about that. This couldn't end any way but bad for me.

But I just couldn't help myself.

Like an idiot, I started to walk toward the gaping mouth of the building, staring up at the cavernous entryway that towered over me. It was so dark inside I couldn't see my hand in front of my face. I smacked right into a wall. Stumbling around with my arms out, I followed that wall and realized it was actually rounded to follow the circular external shape of the dome. It was like an enclosed arena made of solid rock. A structure like this wouldn't be fazed by a dragon's snapping jaws or flashing flames.

A sudden sharp hiss off to my left made me flinch and gasp, spinning around to see there was a faint, golden light trickling from around the corner. It felt far away, and as I walked toward it, I couldn't tell if I was getting any closer or if it was actually moving away from me. A few more steps brought me around the curved inner wall, and there was a sudden thundering roar. It was so loud it rattled the floor, and made me clamp my hands over my ears. I could feel the pulsing under my boots coming from some kind of impact, like when Ulric was working with his hammer and I could feel the ground vibrating under my feet.

The gold light was coming through a half-cracked set of massive iron doors. They towered over me, so big a giant could have used them without having to worry about bumping his head. One of them was open just enough that bright light poured out from within. My heart was hammering in my ears. Something smelled like smoke, and I could still hear the sound of that rumbling growl like thunder.

I'd come too far not to see whatever was making such a racket inside. Inch by inch, I hedged toward the crack in the door, and finally peered in. The light was bright at first, so I had to squint to see. All I saw was a flash of blue scales, and another trumpeting roar made me run for cover behind the heavy door. I was shaking so badly I could barely stand up, and I still wasn't sure what I'd seen in there.

"Get a good look?" An angry voice snapped at me suddenly.

I almost fainted from terror. A big man-shaped shadow was looming over me, standing right behind me. I couldn't think, I couldn't even breathe, and didn't know how to even begin explaining myself.

Then he stepped into the light, and I knew right away who it was. Sile Derrick was frowning down at me with his big, muscular arms crossed over his chest. He wasn't wearing his armor this time, instead he had on a tunic and pants that stank like sweat, and were a little scorched around the corners. He glared down at me like I'd done something terrible, still waiting for an explanation.

"I-I thought I heard ... " I started to speak, but lost my nerve. None of the excuses I could think of sounded even slightly convincing.

He shook his head, frowning harder down at me with his dead eyes narrowed. "Go on, then. Get a good, long look, boy."

I opened my mouth to protest. I didn't really want to see what was in there anymore. I'd seen enough.

He wasn't going to let me off that easy, though. With one of his big hands planted on my shoulder, he steered me around and back toward the crack in the door. Again, the bright light blinded me, and I had to squint to see what was inside. But as I blinked away the glare, I saw the arena.

It was a huge, circular room with a dirt floor and a domed ceiling made out of solid steel with big iron cross beams. It had to be at least thirty—maybe even forty—feet tall, lit by torches that filled the room with golden light. I'd never seen a room so big before, and my mouth was hanging open long before I even saw the dragon.

He saw me at the same time, and our eyes locked

from across the wide arena floor. At first, all I could do was stare at him while he glared back at me. I stopped, terror making my legs go completely stiff even with the powerful knight's hand still gripping my shoulder. I didn't want to go any closer than was absolutely necessary. Part of me was beginning to wonder if my punishment for nosing around would be becoming a late-night dragon snack.

I'd never seen a dragon up close before, but now I was standing only a few yards away from one. He was tied down to the floor with heavy iron chains. His head, neck, wings, legs, and tail were all clamped down to the ground so that he couldn't do much more than snarl at us. And that's exactly what he did.

His big yellow eyes stared right at me, pupils narrowed into slits, and he curled his lips up to snarl. Then I heard that growl again, that thunderous rumble, and all my hair stood on end. I must have gone a few minutes without taking a breath, because I started to feel faint.

"It isn't very often we are able to catch a wild dragon." Sile Derrick was looking at the creature, but he wasn't frowning anymore. He looked almost sad, watching the dragon that was still showing us his rows of pointed teeth. "In the old days, all dragons were born wild. When they chose a rider, they were brought here to be broken to a saddle. It was like a sacred bonding ritual that paired the two forever as allies. That's why they call this place the breaking dome. But now dragons are bred like horses. They don't have a choice about who will become their rider, like they did in the old days. That is—unless we come across a wild one like this."

I'd stopped trembling, and started breathing again. It didn't look like the dragon could move, otherwise we probably would have already been his midnight meal. "Who did he choose?" I wanted to know.

Sile shook his head. "No one. We've tried about twenty different candidates, but he won't even let us put a saddle on him. He's sent a few of them home in crutches, in fact. They were lucky to get away without losing a limb."

I swallowed hard. The dragon blinked at me, giving a loud snort out his nostrils that sent a puff of hot air blasting at my face.

"The Academy Commander has decided he's too dangerous to let anyone else try. He's too old to be ridden. If he were younger, maybe then we could break his spirit enough to let someone ride him. But we can't risk anyone else getting hurt. It's bad enough to have riders die in battle, let alone in training." Sile let his hand slide off my shoulder, and he gave a loud sigh. "I've been trying to reason with him. It's a shame. He'll have his wing tendons cut, most likely, and be used for breeding."

That didn't sit too well with me. He refused to conform, to be broken to the will of a rider, and so they were just going to take away his freedom altogether? Why did they have the right to do that? Hadn't he been born free? The more I looked at the dragon, tied down to the ground and glowering at us with wild fury, the more I understood his anger. He'd never fly again, if these knights got their way.

"If he had a rider," I started to ask. "If someone could ride him, I mean. If it were possible, would he still have to have his wing tendons cut?"

Sile met my gaze as I glanced back up at him. There was a strange twinkle in his dark eyes when he answered, "I'd like to think that if he was willing to take a rider, then there's no reason he couldn't fly forever with the other dragonriders."

I stared back at the dragon again. His yellow eyes were glaring right back at me, but he'd stopped snarling and growling. I saw the end of his tail twitching back and forth, and the way his sides rose and fell under his blue scales as he breathed. "Can I ... can I try?" I didn't even realize I'd asked that out loud.

Sile was very quiet. It made me terrified of what the answer was going to be. I thought he'd probably just laugh at me, call me stupid, and send me on my way. After all, the idea that I would ever be allowed to be a dragonrider was totally ridiculous. Dragonriders came from rich noble families. I was the nobody of nobodies. I was just a halfbreed.

"Move slowly," Sile answered quietly. "And keep looking in his eyes."

I nodded shakily. My legs felt like jelly as I took a step toward the dragon. One step, then another, and the creature looked bigger and bigger the nearer I got to him. His scales were a sapphire color mottled in darker, slate blue. Three sets of horns as black as onyx crowned his head, matching his black claws on his wing arms and hind legs.

When I was only three yards away, his ears perked up in my direction. He had two small, almost feline looking ears that swiveled in my direction for a moment before flattening back against his skull. His snout wrinkled up again, and he let out a low growl of warning. I was too close for his liking.

I couldn't imagine I looked nearly as intimidating as Sile did, or even as any of the other new riders who'd already tried to get on him. I was a scrawny little kid. I'd make a good toothpick for him. But now, I was praying that would work in my favor. If I didn't look like a threat, maybe he wouldn't treat me like one.

"Please," I spoke to him. I didn't think he could understand me. It just made me feel better to talk to him. "I know what it feels like, believe me. They don't know what to do with you. And now they want to keep you here like some kind of prisoner. It's not fair. It's not right."

The dragon kept growling at me, but he didn't move again. I just locked my eyes on his and tried not to think about how close I was to the end of his snout as I kept moving forward. His head was large, much bigger than a horse's, and I could see his nostrils flaring as he breathed in my scent. His scales were larger than some of the other dragons I'd seen already. They shone under the golden torchlight like polished blue steel.

The more I looked at him, the more I noticed his features were sort of feline in shape. He was like a cross between a lizard, housecat, and a bat. His snout was short, and his eyes were large like a cat. The undersides of his hind legs and the thumbs on his wing arms had pads on them, too. His body shape was almost like a bat's, except for the long lizard-like tail and lean muscles rippling under his scales. He had two powerful back legs, but his front ones were connected to his wings. All dragons had that same kind of basic physique, though I hadn't noticed any of the others looking as cat-like in their faces, and I certainly hadn't seen any other blue ones.

"I think we can agree that things are pretty lousy for both of us," I went on talking to him, closing the distance between us. My voice was shaking because I was scared out of my mind, but at least he hadn't made a lunge for me yet. "Let's make a deal, all right? I don't want to keep living with my father for the rest of my life, and I definitely don't want to go to a prison camp. I want my life to mean something. And I'm pretty sure you don't want them to cut your wings so you can't fly anymore. You want them to let you go, but they'll force you to stay here one way or another. Alone, neither of us can do anything to change the way things are going for us. But together, we could change both our destinies."

I was standing so close to him, I could smell the musk of his breath. I could feel it, too, hot and humid against my face. Reaching out, I could see my own hand trembling as I crept toward him. Just a few more feet. Then a few more inches.

"Let me be your rider," I pleaded with him. "I swear I won't make you do anything you don't want to do. And when we're finished, when the war is over, you'll be free to go back to the wild. I won't treat you like a dumb animal. You'll be my partner. We'll get through this together. We'll be a team."

My hand touched his head. My heart felt like it had stopped beating. I could feel his scales under my palm. They were smooth like polished marble, but warm and alive.

The dragon perked his ears again, his snarl finally fading away. He made strange popping, clicking noises like the chattering sparrows did when they squabbled with each other. His yellow eyes stared at me, and his nostrils puffed as I moved my hand down toward his nose, letting him sniff me.

"I swear," I told him, and my voice wasn't shaking anymore. I didn't feel afraid. "You have my word."

Something went skidding across the floor and stopped just beside me. It was a set of iron keys. I looked back at Sile, who was watching with his eyes wide. He looked completely stunned, like he was in awe. He didn't have to explain to me what the keys were for.

I bent to pick them up, moving to the huge black padlock that bound the dragon to hooks in the floor with the heavy chains. I unlocked the one that kept his head flattened against the ground. As soon as it clicked and the chain went slack, the dragon began to flail.

I was too close to get away. The dragon's lashing tail hit me and swept my legs right out from under me, sending me sliding across the floor on my back. I heard the chains groaning and snapping, hitting the ground as the dragon let out a surging bellow of victory. I'd had some near-death experiences before, but this was definitely way worse than any of the others.

Sile was shouting, and I glimpsed him brandishing

what looked like a long spear, running toward me like he was going to try to rescue me again. The dragon wasn't going to allow that, though. With a vicious snarl, he tore off the rest of the chains, and reared back onto his hind legs to open his wings.

He was as fast as he was big, and snapped his head forward when Sile tried to stick him with the spear, grabbing it in his jaws, and snapping it like a twig. The dragon spat out the pieces of the spear, taking a threatening snap at Sile, who was already beginning to retreat.

"Stop! Don't hurt him!" I cried. I didn't expect that to make a spit's worth of difference … but it did.

The dragon stopped, hunkered on all four of his feet, and shot me a glare of pure frustration with those huge cat-like eyes. His tail kept swishing as he sat there, the leathery skin of his wings folded up along his forelegs like a bat, and gave me an angry snort. He made those popping, chattering noises again as he swung his head back around to look at Sile, who looked just as stupefied and shocked as I was.

The dragon was *listening* to me.

"Unbelievable," Sile whispered. I could see his expression twitching, like thoughts were racing across his brain, until at last his gaze panned slowly over to me. He didn't have much color left in his face. "Do it again."

I swallowed hard; I didn't want to try it again. Any time now, my luck was bound to run out. Then I'd be torched with dragon fire, or gobbled up like a kid-shaped biscuit. Gathering my feet under me, I stood back up. The dragon was watching me again, studying my every move.

"If you're really going to make this deal with me, you have to show me," I spoke to the creature again. "Show me that I can trust you."

The dragon turned and started walking toward me. His large, curled black claws dug into the dirt floor of the arena, and I couldn't help but stagger back a few feet as he crept toward me, chattering loudly all the way. His gait was strange to watch, oddly smooth and feline for the way his body was built.

He stopped right before me, craning his neck to sniff at me again. Then he started to crouch down. The dragon lowered himself until his belly was flat on the ground. His huge horned head was low, too, and he looked at me expectantly.

Before I could figure out what I was supposed to do, Sile was right there beside me. "He wants to seal the bond," the knight explained as he grabbed me by the waist and pretty much tossed me up onto the dragon's back. "Don't be afraid."

Easy for him to say; Sile wasn't the one straddling

the neck of a wild dragon who'd already proven he had a nasty temper. With my legs slung around the base of the creature's neck, sitting between the shoulders of his wing arms, I clung to anything I could when I felt him start to move. There wasn't much to grab, though. His scales were slick, and the little knobby black horns that ran down his spine to the tip of his tail were cone-shaped and hard to grip. I just had to lay flat against his neck, my arms as far around him as I could reach, and hung on for dear life as the dragon stood.

Sile was laughing loudly. I saw him smiling up at me as the dragon gave a wide yawn that showed me just how many of those teeth he had. My heartbeat was skipping and pounding erratically. My head spun like a top. I was sitting on a dragon. Not just any dragon, though. This one was *mine*.

four

"You'll be stacking stones over my grave before I allow that repulsive little wretch into this academy! Have you absolutely lost your mind?" The Academy Commander was yelling so loudly I could hear him from outside his office. So could my father, and all the other instructors who had come to gather outside the door. They all wanted to see what the verdict would be, too. If the commander allowed me to join in the training program and become a dragonrider, it would be the first time in history a drop of elven blood had ever been in a dragon's saddle.

Normally, I would have been humiliated. But I was so tired and hungry, I just wanted it to be over. I stood beside Ulric, staring down at the tops of my boots while I listened to Sile Derrick argue my case. For whatever reason, he was still insisting that I should be allowed to join. I didn't understand why. No one else had ever fought for me like that before.

"You'd spit in the faces of our ancestors? On our most sacred tradition?" Sile yelled back. I heard what sounded like someone smacking a fist down onto a tabletop. "This is how we began, Commander Rayken. It is our creed; the very foundation of what this brotherhood was built upon. Any rider chosen by a dragon must be allowed to join us—that is our first law!"

"And what about all our glorious dead who have fallen in battle to those silver-headed heathens? Are you willing to spit in their faces, instead?" The commander started yelling again. It made my throat begin to feel tight. "By letting that boy in here, you are acknowledging that there is nothing wrong with what he is. He would be a stain on the reputation of our brotherhood. I don't care if it was a king drake that chose him. That does not forgive his bloodline!"

There was silence for a moment. I thought it was over. I didn't know whether to be relieved that a decision had finally been reached, happy that I wasn't going to have to endure being bullied by knights who were supposed to be training me, or sad because I wasn't going to get to fulfill what might have been my destiny.

I flicked a glance up to the dozen or so instructors, all ranking officers, who were standing around waiting to hear a decision as well. I was afraid of them. They were all strong, powerful-looking men with the same cold eyes that Sile had. Did I really want to become one of them?

"If you don't let him in, you are sending the message that our old ways really are dead. You'll be suggesting that the spirit of the dragon no longer matters at all, that we've bred them down to stupid beasts no better than winged pedigree dogs!" Sile countered, but his voice was somewhat calmer. It carried more emotion than anger now. "I know you've heard those accusations whispered at our backs, just as I have. They say we've fallen from our glorious past, and become nothing but power-hungry relics without souls. That is not the legacy I want to leave here for the world to remember. That boy can help us change it. We can prove that our heritage is not dead, that we still honor the creed of our forefathers."

"Have you even seen that boy? He couldn't possibly weigh a hundred pounds soaking wet. He won't last two weeks. The other fledglings would be three years his senior. They'll eat him alive." The commander's tone wasn't any less hostile. "You'll be scraping what's left of him off the dormitory walls."

"I'll watch over him," Sile interrupted. "I'll be his sponsor."

"You're a fool, lieutenant. What's come over you? Why does this halfbreed mean so much to you?" The commander sounded suspicious, but he didn't wait for Sile to give him an answer. "What has his father said? Even as a tackmaster, I doubt he has in the income to pay for the equipment needed."

"I'll take care of that, too. If these are your only real objections, then give me your blessing so I can begin my work. I only have two days to get him fully outfitted and ready to begin." Sile snapped sharply.

I heard the commander sigh. It was the sound of defeat. My heart jumped with hope, making my eyes water.

"Very well," he relented. "But you are going to get that boy killed. His blood is on your hands, Lieutenant Derrick. Remember that. You wanted this."

There was a brief silence before the door opened, and Lieutenant Sile Derrick came out of the commander's office. His expression was steely and focused. He didn't give my father a second look as he stormed past the crowd of other knights who were still gathered around. He grabbed my shoulder on his way down the stairs, and started to drag me along with him.

"What are you doing with him?" Ulric barked, lunging forward like he might try to stop us.

Sile stopped at the top of the stairs long enough to

look back, casting my father a look that I'd seen Ulric give me many times; that look of superiority and disgust. "He's no longer your concern, tackmaster. Remember your place."

Ulric's eyes were burning like torches. His fists clenched in rage as Sile pushed me on ahead of him down the stairs. It was surreal, and I wasn't even sure if it was really happening. Just like that, Ulric couldn't put his hands on me anymore. Just like that, I was free.

Or maybe I'd just traded in one horror for another.

I should have been exploding with gratitude for Sile. He'd just fought fiercely so I could stay here and be trained as a dragonrider. But as we paused outside the officer's dormitory, I couldn't help questioning his motives. No one had ever helped me do anything before, and generosity of this magnitude was a foreign concept to me. It was frightening. I barely knew this man, and already I owed him my life.

He seemed to pick up on my hesitance as we walked in silence toward the breaking dome. "Commander Rayken is right, you know. The other students will be at least eighteen. They are probably going to give you a hard time."

I rolled my eyes. "Everyone gives me a hard time, sir. I'm used to that already. That's not what I'm worried about."

"Well, all right then." He laughed under his breath.

"What are you worried about?"

It was hard to pick just one thing. I was worried about my own physical ability. I was worried about owing a stranger my life. And more than anything, I was worried I wouldn't be able to keep my promise to my dragon. If I couldn't make it through this training, then I'd be failing more than just myself. I'd made a deal with that creature, and I wanted to keep my word. Both our lives depended on it now.

"I haven't eaten in about two days," I told him instead. I didn't want to look weak. Well, weak-*er*. "I guess I'm just worried about food, right now."

Sile laughed again, clapping a hand on my back that made me stumble some as I walked beside him. "That we can fix. You look like a scrawny stray cat, boy. Maybe some decent food'll put more meat on your bones."

I blushed. It was embarrassing to have my stature pointed out more than once in a day. "Yeah," I mumbled back. "Maybe."

The dining hall was in the ground level of the student dormitory, and that's where Sile sat me down in front of a tray stacked with roasted meat, freshly baked bread, boiled eggs, and cold milk. My mouth was hanging open. The smells were fantastic, and I seized my fork like a weapon, preparing to go to war with the first thing I could get my hands on.

"Eat up," he commanded. I noticed he wasn't sitting down to join me for this incredible breakfast. "I've got to go get your paperwork filed and put in orders at the armories for your gear. You know where that is, don't you?"

I nodded.

"Good, come straight over when you're finished. We've got some catching up to do." Sile smirked, going on about his business, and leaving me with a fork in my hand and a mountain of food to tackle.

I was too busy stuffing as much into my mouth as I could to realize I was being watched. I gulped down three boiled eggs, shoveled in several big bites of the roasted meat, and drained my glass of milk before I even stopped to breathe.

The food was so good I didn't even notice it when someone came over and sat down across the table from me. There were lots of empty seats in the dining hall. The four long tables stretched from one end of the room all the way to the other, with wooden benches on either side. A few hundred people could have easily sat in the dining hall to eat without being too crowded. So there was really no reason anyone would have sat by me … unless they just wanted to.

I looked across the table into the grinning face of a boy I didn't recognize. He was a lot older than me, maybe eighteen or nineteen, with shaggy dark blonde hair and light brown eyes the color of amber. I got the feeling right away that he was probably going to make fun of me. That's generally how things went. So I braced for the inevitable.

"You keep eating like that and you'll make yourself puke," he said. I watched him reach out to tear a hunk off my loaf of bread and pop it into his mouth. "You must be the new kid."

I sat back away from the table some, still armed with my fork, but not willing to fight him for my food. I could part with a few pieces of bread as long as no one was wiping their boots on my face. "Yeah," I answered hesitantly. "H-how did you know that?"

He just laughed. "It's a small place. Word travels fast here. Especially when it concerns a halfbreed and a wild dragon. And in case you hadn't noticed, you're the only halfbreed here," he pointed out matter-of-factly. "Word is you'll be joining us in the fledgling class in a few days. Guess that means we'll be classmates."

I wasn't sure if I should be talking to him or not. I didn't get the feeling he was going to hurt me, not like I had from the boys who'd beat me up the day before. He looked at me like I was an interesting insect he wanted to mess with, not squash under his heel. Even so, I wasn't sure who I could trust.

"We're both new kids, then." I tried to sound confident, like I wasn't afraid of him.

It made him laugh again, and he stole another piece of bread off my plate. "Right, right. I guess so, huh?" He was chewing loudly, looking at me with a thoughtful expression for an uncomfortable minute before he spoke again. "So what happened to your face?"

I blushed so hard the tips of my ears were burning. Whenever Ulric hit me, it tended to leave hand-shaped bruises on my skin. I bruised easily anyway, and he never held back just because I was a kid. Of course, I'd also cracked my head off the ladder pretty hard. I probably had a nice black eye to show for that, too. And then there was the whole mess with the other older boys. After all that, I probably did look like a walking corpse.

"I fell." I told him guardedly.

He arched a brow at me like he wasn't buying that for a second. "Into a giant foot, apparently. You've got a boot print on your face, you know."

My ears were on fire, and I couldn't stand to look at him much less answer that. I sat with my shoulders hunched and tense, staring down into my lap while he kept picking at my plate. Finally, he stood up and left without saying another word. He sauntered out of the dining hall with a confident swagger in his step. I didn't even know his name.

Stuffing down a few more bites of food, I cleaned up my tray quickly and set out for the armory. The dragons were taking flight from the tops of the high outer wall, already grouping together in patterns as they soared overhead. I could glimpse their riders for a few seconds whenever they swooped past, and see that they were using hand signals to communicate to one another. It was unfathomable to think I'd ever be like that. Dragon or not, I couldn't see myself as one of those powerful armored men. I couldn't see myself as anything.

A familiar thundering growl made me look back over my shoulder just in time to scramble out of the way as my dragon swooped in low to land. He cupped his leathery wings, and only missed crushing me by a few feet as he touched down. He let out a deep bellowing roar. Under the shining light of the morning sun, he was even more fierce and beautiful than he had been the night before. His blue scales gleamed, and his black horns shone like volcanic glass.

"Try not to kill me before we even get started," I grumbled, turning away to continue on toward the armories. I wasn't feeling confident about this at all, anymore. I was beginning to think I'd made a huge mistake by agreeing to this.

The dragon followed me, looming close and making those chattering, bird-like noises as we made our way toward the armory buildings. I was hoping I wouldn't see my father, but I caught a glimpse of him as I searched the workshops for Sile. All the craftsmen were very busy taking orders or measuring riders for saddles and armor. My father was casting molds for saddles, which I'd never actually seen him do before. Thankfully, he didn't look up when I walked past.

Sile was talking to a blacksmith when I finally found him. They were haggling over the cost of vambraces, and I stood by quietly until my dragon finally made an impatient barking noise. That got their attention, and it made me smile a little.

"Hurry up. Stand there," the blacksmith grumbled in a raspy voice. I knew his type well, thanks to Mr. Crookin. Blacksmiths liked to get down to work, no nonsense, and get their money as quickly as possible so they could move on to their next order.

Sile gave me a nod of encouragement, gesturing for me to come close enough for the blacksmith to start working. "Come on, we've got a lot to get done today."

The blacksmith measured me from head to foot, handling me roughly like someone feathering a chicken, and occasionally squeezing an old bruise hidden by my clothes that made me wince. Occasionally, he stopped and wrote down numbers, noting the length of my arms and legs, the circumference of my chest, and the span of my shoulders. It didn't take him long to get all my measurements taken, and then he started handing me pieces of roughly-made test armor to determine how they felt for size.

It took a few tries of different sizes of helmets to find one that didn't fit me like I was just wearing an empty bucket over my head. It had a big number three painted on the front of it, and the blacksmith made a gruff noise of disapproval. "Been a long time since I made a three. You sure you're big enough for this? War is a man's game."

"No," I answered truthfully.

Sile sent me a scolding glare. "He'll be fine. Size and strength are not all that make a good soldier."

Once I'd been fitted for armor, and the smith had been paid, we moved on to a workstation in the second building—the one where the tackmasters were making saddles. Sile, in all his wisdom, had decided not to hire my father to make mine. Judging by the last look my father had given me, I wouldn't have been surprised if Ulric intentionally compromised my saddle on the off chance that it might kill me.

My dragon followed us to the open-sided workspace, plopping down onto his haunches outside and beginning to preen his scales. The tackmaster was a man much older than my father, with snowy white hair, and knobby withered hands that were covered in protruding veins.

He took one look at me, at my dragon, and his bushy brows shot up for a moment. But he didn't say anything.

"Are you ready for us yet?" Sile talked to the man like he'd already struck a bargain with him.

The old tackmaster nodded. "Have the dragon lie down."

All eyes were suddenly on me, expecting me to get my dragon to perform like a trained show pony. I swallowed hard. I wasn't sure just how much of what I said the dragon actually understood, or how smart he was. It was time to find out.

As I walked up to his head, my dragon was watching me with large yellow eyes bright with what I hoped was intelligence. I raised a hand to him, showing him my palm, and then gesturing in a downward motion. "Lie down, will you?" I asked him nicely. It was strange to give something that huge, and that potentially deadly, orders.

The dragon watched my gesture, and made a few soft clicking noises as he canted his head to one side. His ears perked and swiveled.

"Down," I repeated. "Lie down."

He was already sitting back on his haunches, and little by little, he started to lower himself until he was lying flat on his scaly belly. He watched me carefully the whole time, looking for indication that he was doing the right thing.

"Yes, that's right." I couldn't keep myself from grinning. Even if he didn't understand me word for word, my dragon was smart. He could figure out what I wanted. "Good."

Sile was impressed again. He watched us with his arms folded, and I saw a glimmer of envy in his eyes when I turned back to face him. "You think of a name for him yet?"

I glanced back at my dragon, who was still watching me intently as he lay still. Naming him hadn't even crossed my mind yet. "No. How do other riders usually choose names?"

"Well, these days young dragons are named after their sires, or mothers, whichever was the more impressive specimen." Sile grabbed the back of my shirt while he talked, pulling me out of the blacksmith's way as he began dragging one of the large molds toward my dragon.

The old blacksmith worked slowly, but he was strong like my father, and he didn't act like he wanted us to help him. He, like all tackmasters, had his own way of doing things. For these men, I knew making saddles was a sacred ritual. He wouldn't want us to interfere.

Standing back with Sile, we watched the old smith work at pressing the wax-filled mold against the space between my dragon's neck and his wing arms, where the saddle would sit. The mold would become the base that the rest of the saddle would be built to fit onto, so that it was snug against the dragon's body and didn't slide around. It also had to fit over the little horns growing down his spine.

"You know, the other instructors had started calling him a maverick. For a wild-born dragon who refused all but a halfbreed rider, that name might suit him," Sile muttered.

"Maverick?" I wasn't sure what that meant.

Sile was smirking to himself while he studied my dragon with his dark eyes. "A rebel. That's what it means. That's what he is. A stubborn mongrel, albeit a smart one."

I liked the way that named sounded. It rang well, and when I looked at the blue-scaled dragon lying on his belly, yawning widely to show us his white teeth and black gums, it just seemed to fit him. I took up a stick and squatted down to scribble the letters into the dirt at my feet.

M-A-V-R-I-K.

"You didn't spell it right." Sile was grinning at me, and shaking his head.

I looked up at him, then back down at the name. Spelling had never been my strong suit. My mother had taught me to read pretty well, but I'd never had much need for writing.

"It's fine, boy." Sile squatted down next to me to get a closer look at the name I'd scribbled in the dirt. "Mavrik. I like it spelled that way. What do you think, dragonrider? Is that the name for him?"

I couldn't keep from smiling back at the older knight who had quickly become my closest friend. Well, besides Katty, anyway. A little glowing bit of warmth started to rise up in my chest, and it made me want to smile even wider. When I looked at my dragon, at Mavrik, I started to feel that sensation bloom out all over my body. It was like a rush of energy and hope.

"Yeah, I think so."

five

It'd been a long day. After getting all my armor and my saddle ordered, my admission paperwork signed and submitted, and making sure Mavrik was settled in at the Roost, all I wanted to do was sleep. I didn't even care where anymore.

Sile left me standing outside the student dormitory with a stack of books and uniforms in my arms. "Your room is on the second floor," he told me as he turned away. "Students have to share a room with one other person their first year. He'll be your partner in training for the duration. It supposedly promotes comradery, though in your case, I'd advise you to keep a low profile. Room four."

My spirits fell. I was going to have a roommate. A partner. Sile had explained a lot about how the first year of training was going to work. There were nine students starting, including me. All were boys. Girls weren't allowed to become dragonriders. So, odds were, I was going to end up in a room with someone that hated my guts. There was only one boy from my new class that had even been remotely nice to me—while he was stealing food off my plate. I knew chances were slim that he would end up being my roommate, but I would have happily roomed with a food thief than someone else who might want to beat me within an inch of my life.

I dragged my feet up the stairs to the second floor of the student dormitory. The hallways were narrow, with rows of doors on either side. I stopped outside door number four, staring up at the engraved lettering hanging on a placard in the very middle of it. It read:

4
Sn. Lt. Derrick

The other doors had signs on them, too, and from what I could tell each one had the name of a Lieutenant on it. That must have been what Sile meant by being my "sponsor." Even if I wasn't sure what a sponsor was, I was glad that I'd at least be in some proximity to the knight who'd vouched for me.

I had just reached out to touch the doorknob, when I heard a familiar voice snarl behind me, "You've got to be kidding me."

I recognized the older boy right away. It was the same one who'd wiped his boots on my face. He was glaring at me like he'd found a diseased rodent in his food, and immediately I froze up. He was bigger than me, and I knew I wouldn't stand much of a chance if he came after me again. I could run, but I wouldn't get far.

"There's no way!" He yelled like it was my fault. Apparently Sile was his sponsor, too. "I'll cut my own ears off before I share a room with you!" He was practically screaming, and I started to worry about what he was going to do to me.

He started to move in closer, backing me up against the door while he snapped angry words just inches from my nose. I couldn't escape, and I couldn't think of anything to say to defend myself. The more furious he got, the louder he became, and it made me wince as I tried to hide behind the stack of supplies in my arms.

Some of the other new students were starting poke their heads out of their rooms down the hall, staring at us. I could sense their anticipation as they started to flock toward us. They were hoping for a fight. It would be a free-for-all, and I would definitely be on the losing end of it. Every single one of them was at least half a foot taller than I was, and much more muscular. I was a sheep surrounded by a pack of hungry wolves, ready to make a meal of me.

"Hey," another, strangely familiar voice spoke up from within the crowd. I watched the other students step aside, making way for the boy who'd stolen bites of my lunch earlier. He was coming straight for us with a canvas bag slung over his shoulder.

"I'll switch with you," he said "I'll room with the halfbreed."

My mouth fell open.

"Well if it isn't the local celebrity, Felix Farrow. Come to see how the other half lives?" The boy was still snarling in my direction with his eyes narrowed, bowing up defensively at the one who'd interrupted his fit of rage. "What does the son of a duke want with a halfbreed, anyway?"

"The way I see it, that's not really any of your business, is it?" Felix shot him a threatening look. "You want to switch or not? This offer's going to last for about thirty more seconds."

It didn't take that long for him to make up his mind. The boy who had used my face as a doormat agreed to switch rooms without any more yelling, and he sent me a mocking sneer over his shoulder as he walked away.

The crowd started to disperse, as everyone went back into their rooms, seeming unhappy that things hadn't come to blows. I was left standing alone in the hallway with Felix Farrow, wondering what had just happened. How had I gotten out of that situation with all my limbs and teeth intact?

Felix gave me a look from top to bottom like he was sizing me up, and then he just rolled his eyes. "You've got a knack for getting in trouble. Let's hope that doesn't apply to the battlefield, too."

I didn't know what to say to him except, "Thank you."

He just shrugged and opened the dorm room door, holding it so I could go in first.

"Is Sile going to be all right with this?" I wasn't sure switching like this was allowed.

He gave me a strange look. "You mean Lieutenant Derrick?"

I nodded. "Yeah. Will he be your sponsor now, too?"

"First off, you can't call him that anymore, kid." Felix corrected me as he shut the door behind us. He wandered over to one of the two single beds set up on opposite sides of the room. He plopped his canvas bag there, claiming it as his own. "He's Lieutenant Derrick to us. We're not on a first name basis with our superior officers. Understand? That'll get you smacked upside the head. Whatever relationship with him you had before, it ends the minute you put on your uniform. He's your sponsor; he's responsible for making sure you survive this training. That's his job. Private training, individualized attention, and providing you with anything you need that your parents didn't already give you."

"Oh, right." I nodded again.

Felix unbuttoned his bag and started taking out his own books and uniforms, putting them away into a small bedside table with a few drawers in it. "And to answer your question, yes. I'll have to talk to him about it to make sure it's all right, but I'm pretty sure they won't care. In fact, I'm willing to bet Lieutenant Derrick will be glad that you're not rooming with Lyon. I heard he was the one who bruised your face up."

I sank down to sit on my own bed, watching him unpack from across the room. I'd never had a bed like this before. It was just a single-sized, hard mattress covered in a stiff white sheet and wool blanket, but it was still nicer than anything I'd ever had before.

"Is that his name? Lyon?" I asked while I unfolded one of my uniform shirts to look at it. It was just a plain, dark blue tunic with a golden eagle stitched on the breast. It was made of a coarse, rugged fabric, and the sleeves were long enough to be tucked into my vambraces, whenever I got them.

"Lyon Cromwell," Felix confirmed. "Son of Viscount Cromwell, and a third generation rider in his family."

Hearing that made my spirits sink some. I hadn't even had my first day of training yet, and I was already making powerful enemies. I looked up at Felix, who was still busy putting his things away. "Why did you do that?" I dared to ask. "Why did you agree to switch? No one else wants anything to do with me."

He stopped long enough to give me another strange look, arching one of his eyebrows. I knew he was a noble, too. I'd heard Lyon call him the son of a duke, and that was just a step below a prince. He definitely had that rich kid look about him. His dark blonde hair was cut feathery around his face, and his clothes were clean and expensive-looking. He even had a gold signet ring on his hand with his family crest on it.

"You think I should be worried about my reputation?" He asked.

"Well." I was hesitant to answer that. "I think anyone else would be."

Felix gave a noisy sigh and came around to sit on the edge of his bed, too, staring at me while he sat across the room. "I don't know," he admitted. "I'm sure my dad's not going to like it, but he doesn't like a lot of things I do. Besides, you're interesting. A halfbreed paired with a wild-caught dragon? Maybe I'm just waiting to see what amazing, unexpected thing you do next."

I was able to smile at him some, glancing back down at the uniform tunic in my hands. "Like what? Surviving a year of dragonrider training at Blybrig Academy?"

Felix laughed loudly, grinning at me in that same mischievous way he had when I first met him. "Yeah, exactly like that."

The dormitory was dark and quiet once we were all settled in. Felix was already snoring in his bed, when I got back from the washroom down the hall. I hadn't had an opportunity to bathe in almost a week, and probably stank to high heaven. I finally got a chance to look at myself in the mirror behind the washstand before I left. Now I understood why Felix had asked about my bruises. Some were green and healing, but others were still deep purple. I could trace the outline of Ulric's hand on one of my cheeks, and a boot print on my forehead.

I hated seeing my reflection. It reminded me just how different I looked from everyone else. If I combed my hair just right, no one could see my slightly pointed ears. But you could still tell I was a halfbreed, even without that. My features were a little sharper, and my cheekbones were high. Katty always told me I had a pretty face, and somehow that never made me feel any better about it.

Crawling under the stiff sheets of my bed, I curled up and tried to sleep. It didn't come easy, though, even if I was exhausted. Felix snored loudly, and sometimes mumbled in his sleep. I couldn't get over the sinking, swirling panic that made me made me sick at my stomach whenever I thought about what I was about to do. I still wasn't sure I was cut out to be a dragonrider. Lieutenant Derrick had faith in me, obviously. He was paying for all my gear, after all, and had agreed to be my sponsor. Mavrik had faith in me, too, or he wouldn't have agreed to pair up with me. I didn't want to disappoint either of them.

The night passed slowly, and I stayed awake rubbing the necklace my mother had given me while I stared at the shadows on the walls from the moonlight outside. It was hard not to miss her. I wondered if she'd be proud of me.

Early in the morning, I heard the trumpet sound that signaled it was time to get up. It wasn't even sunrise yet. I hadn't slept much, so I was still tired. I moved sluggishly to get up and start dressing.

Felix, on the other hand, popped out of bed like he'd been bucked off a horse. I couldn't figure out how he'd even heard the trumpet over his own snoring. He started scrambling to get dressed, putting on the same dark blue tunic and black pants that matched my uniform. Neither of us had vambraces yet, but he had a belt that he buckled around his waist before he sat down to put on his boots.

"Don't you have a sword belt?" he asked me.

I shook my head, wondering if Lieutenant Derrick had forgotten to get me one. He probably hadn't expected he'd have to provide me an entire wardrobe.

"Here." Felix rummaged around through his belongings, tossing me a spare.

I'd never worn a sword belt before. It was way too big, and I had a hard time getting it to fit like I thought it should have. Finally, Felix came over with a sigh to help me.

"Looks like puberty forgot all about you, huh?" He chuckled as he punched a new hole through the belt so it would fit me without falling off. "How old are you anyway?"

I told him, and he just stared at me like I'd grown a third eyeball.

"Geez." He made a sympathetic whistling noise. "You really are just a kid."

"My name is Jaevid," I told him with a frown. I was getting tired of being referred to as just a halfbreed or a kid. I was both, yes, but I had a name.

Felix smirked. "Jaevid, huh?"

"Or just Jae," I added.

He laughed as he stood back, eying the belt like he was trying to make sure it looked good. "You've got boots, right?"

"Yeah." I nodded, and sat down on the edge of my bed to start putting them on.

"Good, cause I don't think my spares would fit you anyway." Felix started talking while he cleaned up his side of the room, advising me to do the same once I was dressed. "They do random room inspections, so you better have all your stuff put away. Uniforms have to be folded neatly, boots by the bedside if you aren't wearing them. Your bed has to be made, books stacked up, and no trash on the floor. Pretty standard stuff."

I started cleaning my side while he talked, not that there was much to clean. I put my clothes and books away, and followed him down toward the dining hall on the first floor. He grabbed a large piece of bread, breaking it in half and shoving some in my direction. He ate while he rushed me out into the cold morning air, talking around the food in his mouth.

Felix explained that official training wouldn't start for a few more days, when everyone finally had all the gear that was being made for us. But this was our chance to get a leg up on the others and start getting some preliminary training from our sponsor.

Lieutenant Derrick was outside the Roost, fitting a saddle to his own dragon. I recognized it was the saddle my father had made for him. The gleaming white creature flared the fins on the side of her head when she saw us coming close, hissing and snapping her jaws. It made Sile look back, arching a brow questioningly at us as we approached. For once, I wasn't the one he narrowed his eyes at, like he was expecting some kind of explanation.

"Felix Farrow, sir." My new roommate introduced himself, clasping a fist over his chest and bowing at the waist. "There was some trouble with room arrangements, and I volunteered to switch…with your permission, of course."

Sile did look at me then. It made me flinch. I didn't know what to say.

"I suppose," Lieutenant Derrick answered hesitantly. "If that's what you want."

Felix nodded. "Yes sir, I'm sure. With all due respect, I'm probably the only one who isn't going to try to snap his skinny neck during the night." He laughed tensely.

Sile gave a snort, but didn't answer. He went back to fixing the saddle onto his dragon. The beautiful, sleek female had scales like polished pearl. Her eyes were a pale, glacier blue and she looked at us like we were something to eat. She wasn't as big as Mavrik, and her build was more lithe. She hissed at me again, her wild eyes turning away when Sile gave her neck a slap.

"Well, I'm glad you've both come," he announced, turning back to face us. "Every morning, I expect you to meet me here before sunup. You'll be doing drill rides, once you get your saddles. You'll be running in full armor, four laps around the outer wall. There is a reason dragonriders are the preferred soldier of his majesty, the king. We are an elite breed. We are held to a higher standard of performance—one you have only just begun to appreciate. I expect the very best from you at all times. It isn't lineage or bloodlines that make men good soldiers, it is sweat and blood. I can assure you, you'll be drenched in both before your time at this academy is over."

Felix wasn't smiling or laughing anymore. I was horrified.

"For today, I'll be taking you up one at a time for a demonstrational ride, then you can get to running those laps. It'd be in your best interest to get over your air sickness now, so you aren't throwing up on your first day of formal aerial maneuvers." Sile went on, curling a finger at me to call me forward. "You're up first, Jaevid."

I didn't want to go anywhere near him, the saddle, or the snarling white dragon that was swishing her long tail. But I had no choice now. I staggered forward, watching as Sile gave the seat of the saddle a pat. It looked intimidating, and much too small for two people.

He gave his dragon a hand signal and she put her belly on the ground, lowering so we could climb onto her back. I was practically sitting in Sile's lap, which was awkward and uncomfortable. Clearly this saddle wasn't made for two people. It felt like I might fall off as soon as we got moving.

Sile was a little more secure in his seat, with his legs put down into two sheath-like leather sleeves build into the saddle. They came up to his knees, fitting like boots. I saw what they were meant for; those leg-holsters were what would keep him in the saddle when his dragon turned at awkward angles in the sky. I was shaking all over as Sile showed me the handles on either side of the saddle.

"I won't let you fall," he assured me as he belted a leather harness around my shoulders that literally strapped us together. It was like he was wearing me as a backpack in the front. "Valla will go easy on you, at first."

Valla didn't seem to like me being on her back one bit. When she stood, she shifted and shook herself, flexing her shoulders and snapping her jaws like my added weight was uncomfortable for her. She growled and hissed, making flustered chirps as she turned her head to the side to glare at me with one big, blue eye.

Sile gave her neck a pat again, gave a sharp whistle, and she reared back onto her hind legs, spreading her forearms wide to flare her wings. I saw Felix stumbled back a few feet as she let out a shrill roar, and leapt skyward. The earth fell away from beneath us, and the sudden force of gravity on my body smashed me back against Sile's chest.

I'd experienced fear a few times, but this was my first encounter with sheer terror. I didn't handle it very well. It took everything I had not to throw up as we rocketed up into the sky. The initial ride was so rough I was afraid something was wrong. Valla took in forceful sweeps with her wings. It felt clumsy and chaotic, like we weren't making any progress, until I caught a glimpse of the ground far below.

She leveled off once we were several hundred feet above the academy, circling at a gentle speed. Looking down made me dizzy, and I was gripping the handles so tightly my hands felt numb. The air was cold, and the sky above was pink as the sun began to rise. I could still see stars peeking through the twilight.

That's when I realized how beautiful it was, and I forgot all my fears.

To the right, I could see where the mountains sloped down, opening to let in a view of the ocean far away in the distance. The rest of the way around us, the peaks of the mountains were still covered in snow. Sile pointed over my shoulder, showing me a few dark spots in the distance. There were other dragons already flying with their riders.

My feelings of awe and exhilaration lasted for about three minutes. Once I had finally gotten comfortable, maybe even decided this was kind of fun, Sile turned up the speed again. He gave Valla another nudge, and with a few forceful wing beats, we went lurching forward.

We did spins. We did spirals. We went up so fast all I could see was blue sky and blurs of clouds. We went down so suddenly I lost my breath and couldn't catch it again until we'd slowed down. All the while, Sile was trying to shout directions at me, and I couldn't understand anything he said with the wind in my face.

Swooping back down toward the earth, Valla cupped her wings and hovered for a moment while she stretched out her strong hind legs and landed. We came to a sudden lurching halt, and immediately I felt like I was going to throw up.

I barely made it out of the saddle in time. Sile must have heard me gagging, because he frantically started unbuckling the harness that tethered us together. He all but dropped me out of the saddle, and as soon as I hit the ground, I started throwing up. When I finally pulled myself together and looked up, Felix as standing over me with a look of horror on his face; now it was his turn.

I sat in the shade while Felix had his demonstrational ride. It still felt like the world was spinning around me. Sile had given me a canteen of water, and told me to keep drinking until I felt better. When they landed again, my head had finally started to clear, but I was still really embarrassed that I'd actually gotten motion sick.

Until Felix threw up, too.

He seemed all right, at first. He unbuckled, got down, and staggered a few feet. He was even grinning, and giving me a thumbs up. Then I saw his face get really pale, his eyes went wide, and he hunched over to puke in the grass just like I had.

Sile was laughing when he got out of the saddle, shaking his head at us and wrinkling his nose at the smell. "Looks like you boys have a lot to get used to." He chuckled, giving me a nod. "Let him drink some, too. Take a few minutes, then you both have laps to run. Meet me again in the dining hall for lunch after you've cleaned yourselves up."

six

Four laps around the outer wall of the academy was about the equivalent of four miles. It probably doesn't sound like much, but for someone who'd never run that far just for exercise, it was pure torture. My legs ached, my lungs felt like someone with big fists was squeezing them shut, and I was soaked with sweat.

Felix seemed to handle it much better. He ran behind me the whole time, and gave me a shove if I slowed down too much. I knew if I stopped, he'd drag me by the ears if he had to. I couldn't imagine what it was going to be like to run those laps in full armor.

As we rounded the last corner on our final lap, I was limping because my calves felt like they were about to pop off the back of my legs. I was starving, dripping sweat, and ready to lie back down and sleep the whole afternoon away. But Sile had a full day planned for us.

We hurried through bathing, changing into clean uniforms, and getting back down to the dining hall. It was a little after noon, so there were a lot of other students and instructors eating while we sat and waited for Sile.

Felix plopped down across from me at one of the long tables, bringing a tray he'd piled high with food for us to share. "Eat while you can," he said as he grabbed a leg of roasted chicken for himself from one of the plates. "I bet we're about to get a jump start on some academics."

I groaned, hesitantly taking a loaf of bread and piece of fruit for myself. "I guess if my brain is hurting, too, it'll take some of the focus off my legs."

He laughed with his mouth full. "Get used to it. We've got two whole years of this ahead of us now."

Even after everything I'd been through so far: the aches, the pain, even the throwing up—hearing that still made me smile somehow. This was going to be the most difficult thing I'd ever done, but it was the first time in my life I'd ever felt like I was doing something worthwhile. It was the first thing that ever promised any kind of future for me.

Sile finally joined us after we'd eaten, sitting down and dumping a pile of maps onto the table between us.

They smelled musty, and were made of thick parchment that had been crinkled and weathered from use. He started to spread some out on the table, using cups and plates to hold them out flat.

"Meet your new best friend," Sile announced, sitting back so we could lean in and get a good look. "You're only useful if you know where you are, and where you need to be. In and out of the saddle, knowing your maps is vital. You'll spend more time with your nose pressed against this paper than doing anything else. In a week, I expect you both to be able to duplicate this purely out of memory."

My jaw dropped. The map was so detailed, I had no idea how we'd ever be able to memorize it all. It wasn't just a map of the valley; it was a map of the entire kingdom of Maldobar. I'd never actually seen a map of it before, and my eyes were immediately drawn across the paper at all the details written with black ink.

Maldobar was a very large peninsula, bordering the sea on the east, west, and south sides. There were forests, rivers, streams, mountains, cities, roads, islands, and even the small desert in the bottom. Every feature had a name, and was labeled in curled writing. There were also different elevations noted in various places, mostly in the mountain regions.

To the north was the forbidding wall of forest labeled

with only one word: Luntharda. I stared at it. It was just a solid mass of forest that covered the whole top part of Maldobar, cutting it off from the rest of the continent. The Wild Forest. The kingdom of the gray elves. That was where my mother had come from, and it was the same kingdom Maldobar had been at war with for so many years.

Sile explained to us about the various markings on the map key, letting us ask questions while he ate his lunch. We discussed the features of the mountains, flying at the different elevations, and the four watch posts where we might get deployed when we finished training. Northwatch was by far the most dangerous, since it was only a few miles from the border of Luntharda. Sile said that was where all new riders had to go if they wanted to earn their stripes.

Finally Felix sat back and let out a noisy sigh. "So what starts first? I mean, as far as training goes. Where do we even begin?"

Sile sat back in his seat some, glancing between us as he folded his arms across his chest. "Boys, this is as much a mind game as it is a test of physical strength and stamina. You'll be stretched beyond your limits every single day. You're going to feel like you're drowning, but just don't let yourself give up. I expect you to get up before the call to arms in the morning." He paused, and glanced at me with a meaningful prick of his brow. "That's the morning horn blast. You run the drills I told you about, in the air and on the ground. I'll show you the flight pattern on your first official day—you probably won't have your saddles by then, so you'll have to piggy back for a while. You need to be back at the breaking dome for your morning brief right after the call to arms. Then you'll head to the gymnasium after the brief for your first lessons in ground combat training. That will take up the first half of your day, so be prepared."

Felix snorted, "Yeah. I've heard about that. They're going to beat the basics into us, right?"

"We all start at the bottom as fledglings. In this brotherhood, respect must be earned." Sile shrugged. It made me wonder what kind of respect he'd won for himself. I didn't know what he'd been through, or what battles he'd fought. I didn't really know much about him at all, except that he had a strange interest in my future.

"You'll be allowed to break for lunch, and then you'll report to the Roost for basic flight patterns and maneuvers. Although, on your first few days, you'll probably be learning how to actually put a saddle on your dragon." Sile smirked like that was funny to him. I could understand why the idea of watching me try to wrestle a big saddle that weighed more than I did onto the back of a wild, ornery dragon might be amusing to someone else. It made me sick to my stomach, though. "Your afternoons will be spent in classes learning the language of hand signals we use in the air, and of course, studying your maps."

"Can't wait." Felix was grinning. He actually looked happy about all this, like he couldn't wait to get started.

Sile just rolled his eyes. "We'll see how you feel about it after your first week. Unless you're psychotic, you'll be writing your mother begging her to let you come back home to your soft, warm bed."

As we settled back into our room for the night, Felix was especially chatty. I could tell he was really excited from our talk with Sile. He went on about his own dragon, a female he'd named Novalla. He called her Nova for short, and told me she was bigger than most females he'd ever seen bred.

"You'll like her," he promised with a wide grin. "She's like a lazy housecat, once you get to know her. I bet she'll get along with yours. What's his name?"

"Mavrik," I answered as I shucked off my boots.

Felix couldn't sit still for a second. He was sitting, then he was up and laying out his gear, then he was looking for his maps, and then he was back sitting on the bed again. I couldn't believe he still had any energy left at all, after what we'd been through all day.

"So, tell me about yourself," he demanded. "I don't

know anything about you, well, except that you've somehow landed in the last place in the world I'd ever expect to see a halfbreed. We're going to be roommates for the next two years, so we might as well get to know one another."

"What is it you want to know?" I looked at him from across the room.

He'd gotten up again, and was obsessively adjusting the laces on his boots. "Well," he spoke without looking up. "Your dad is Ulric Broadfeather, right? The tackmaster?"

I frowned. Already I could tell this was going to be an uncomfortable conversation for me. "Yeah, that's him."

"What about siblings? Or is it just you?"

I told him about Roland and the twins, who were my half siblings. There wasn't much to tell, really. Roland was rarely around, and I'd made a point to avoid Emry and Lin at all costs.

"I never had any brothers or sisters," Felix said as he put one boot down and started working on the other. "My dad popped off a son right away, which is all he wanted, and that was it for kids. He's not exactly a family man. He comes around to tell me when I'm doing something wrong, or when I've embarrassed the family name somehow, but beyond that … we don't really know each other."

Felix and I had more in common than I'd anticipated. Or at least, it was starting to sound that way. "Yeah, Ulric doesn't really like me." I couldn't keep from laughing some at that. It was a huge understatement. "Actually, I'm pretty sure he hates me."

"What about your mom? I mean your real one, not your stepmom," he asked. "What's she like?"

I hesitated. No one had ever asked me about her before. She was obviously where the elven half of my blood had come from, so generally people avoided acknowledging she'd ever existed. I looked up at him warily, and wondered if this was going to end with me having to defend her honor.

Felix met my gaze, waiting for my reply with a curious arch to his brow. "What?"

I looked away quickly, and shrugged. "She's dead." I decided to be vague.

"Did she have a name?" He wasn't going to let me off with that pitiful answer.

"Alowin," I answered reluctantly.

"Well, I'm sorry to hear she's gone." He actually sounded sincere. "You must miss her."

I just bobbed my head. It hurt to talk about her. My memories of her were precious, and I didn't want to share them with anyone I thought might smear her name or accuse her of something she'd never done. People had called her a witch before, or worse.

"So," Felix started to speak again, and I could tell by his voice that he was changing the subject. "On to the important stuff. Girls. You have one in the pocket back at home?"

"What?" I gawked at him. That was ridiculous, but for some reason, it made my face started to burn with embarrassment. "No, of course not."

"You sly pup." He grinned at me cunningly. "You do! Look at you, blushing like an idiot. What's she like, eh?"

I tried to glare at him, to look convincingly resentful of his accusations. But it was no use. "She's just my friend. It's not like that at all."

"Oh sure." He rolled his eyes. Putting his shoes aside, he leaned forward where he sat on the edge of his bed. He looked very interested in what he thought was my love life. "A name, Jae. She's got one, doesn't she?"

"Katalina," I grumbled back. "Really, she's just a friend. I didn't even get to say goodbye to her before I left to come here. She probably thinks I'm dead."

"Dead? Pfft, yeah right." Felix finally started to settle in for the night, kicking back onto his bed, and getting comfortable. "Just write her a letter. Tell her what happened, that you're staying here for a while to be a dragonrider. I bet she'll be after you like flies on flop, then. It just kills the girls, you know."

"What does?" I wasn't sure what he meant by all that, or if I even wanted Katalina to be after me.

"The dragonrider bit," he answered like I should have known that already. "You don't get it do you?"

No, I definitely didn't.

"The ladies love us, Jae. We're the heroes. We're the ones all the other foot soldiers, knights, and cavalrymen *wish* they were. We're masters of the sky, the best of the best, and believe me … the ladies know it. They can't get enough of us."

He jumped out of his bed again, looking at me with a huge grin on his face, and that light of mischief wild in his eyes. "Picture this: the annual officer's ball, and all the big names are there. We're talking generals, colonels, knights, and everyone who's anyone. Of course, all the nobles come to pay their respects, and they bring their dainty little daughters with them to go husband shopping. They're all dolled up and looking for a hero's arm to hang on. Sure, the ground men and cavalry boys can show them a few scars, talk up a few stories, but as soon as *we* hit the doorway—everything changes."

I wasn't convinced. At least, not for my own sake. Sure, I could see rich noble girls going after someone like Felix. He was a dragonrider, and he was also a duke's son. Dragon or not, I was still just a halfbreed. I couldn't imagine noble girls flocking to dance with a bruised up, scrawny halfbreed who was three years younger than all the other students in my class. Girls, even the ones my age, were pretty much always taller than me, anyway.

Felix seemed to be able to tell that I wasn't buying it. He just kept grinning as he lay back down onto his bed, putting his hands behind his head, and chuckling under his breath. "Write a letter to your little sweetheart, and you'll see that I'm right."

seven

The days all started to blur together. We started every morning the same way. We were up before the call to arms, on our feet, and flying drill patterns with Sile. Then we were running laps, and studying our maps. I wish I could say that the longer I kept up that routine, the easier it got. But that wasn't the case. Being in Sile's saddle still made me airsick. The way his dragon flew felt so chaotic to me. Things always started out all right, and then before I knew it, the ground was swirling in my vision and I was back on my hands and knees throwing up. Running was still difficult. Felix kept after me, though, and wouldn't let me fall behind too far. Studying came easier once Sile showed us a strategy of dividing the map up into quadrants to memorize in smaller chunks.

One night Felix caught me trying to write a letter to Katty. After some teasing, he actually helped me with it. My spelling was horrible, or so he said, and he started showing me the mistakes and format for writing a letter. He told me he'd had tutors and scholars teaching him all his life. Actually, he was a pretty good teacher himself.

We kept up that schedule right up until our gear and armor was finally finished. It was the day before training was supposed to start, and Sile told us to meet him at the smithing armory first. A different blacksmith had made Felix's armor, so we weren't together when we got fitted.

I stood on the dressing block while the old blacksmith from before put the different pieces of armor on me over the layer of black thermals I'd been given. Sile stood by, watching, and making comments about the fit being too loose.

"Not my fault," the blacksmith rasped in his raspy voice. "It's like dressing a scarecrow."

The chestplate fit against the top part of my torso, and it was as simple as the light colored steel it was made of. It didn't have any of the ornate designs and engravings I'd seen on Sile's armor before. In fact, none of my armor did. It even felt like I was missing some pieces. I only had the chestplate, gauntlets, vambraces, greaves on my legs, and a helmet. They were all very plain, and felt clunky when I moved.

The helmet was the most interesting to me. It had one long slit across the front where my eyes were so I could see, and there was a thin pane of cut clear glass fitted into it. It was like a miniature window built into the helmet.

"So the wind doesn't mess with your vision," Sile explained when he saw me looking at it.

"Are there pieces missing?" I finally had the nerve to ask.

Sile shook his head, taking the helmet from me to look it over before he crammed it back down on top of my head again. "For now, this is all you need. You're just a fledgling, so there's no need for full battle dress. Don't worry, no one else will have a full set of armor yet, either."

"Oh," I answered. My voice echoed inside the steel helmet.

"Besides, I'm hoping puberty remembers you at some point in the next year. Then we'll have to order a whole new set to be made," he added.

He wasn't the only one hoping that. I wasn't even worried so much about getting taller anymore, even though that would have certainly helped. Now, I just wished for a little more muscle mass. Anything at all, even a pound, would have made me look less like a joke.

On our way out of the armory, I caught a glimpse of

a familiar face out of the corner of my eye. There were a lot of blacksmiths working with riders, and I hadn't even thought about the fact that Mr. Crookin would be there until I saw him talking with an older student. Without thinking, I broke away from Sile and bolted toward him. I didn't have Katty's letter with me, but now I had the perfect way to make sure it got to her.

"Mr. Crookin!" I called out to him, my voice still echoing under my helmet.

He looked down at me, seeming confused by the sight of me until I took the helmet off. Then his eyes got wide, and he put down the hammer he'd been using. "What are you doing, boy? Does Ulric know where you are?"

"Not exactly." I gave him a strained smile. It was a lot to explain. "I'm staying here. I'm going to be a dragonrider."

His eyebrows shot up, and then furrowed down like two bushy storm clouds over his eyes. He glared at me like he was silently accusing me of lying, but one look over my armor was testament that either I was telling the truth, or someone was funding a very elaborate hoax. He just shook his head, and there was a look of restrained sympathy on his face, then. "Jaevid, I don't think you understand what you're getting yourself into."

I didn't really. But I wasn't ready to admit that just

yet. "I wrote a letter to Katty. Would you please take it to her when you go back home? I never got to tell her what happened, or where I went. I didn't get a chance to tell her goodbye, and I don't want her to think I'm dead."

He eyed me again, seeming skeptical, but finally rolled his eyes and nodded. "Put it in my saddle bag before I go. She'll find it."

I smiled and thanked him, preparing to go back to where Sile was waiting, watching me with his arms crossed in disapproval.

As I turned to go, Mr. Crookin barked out another word. "Jaevid."

I stopped and glanced back.

Mr. Crookin's eyes flicked past me, seeing Sile standing there waiting. When he looked back at me, it was like I was as good as dead. "Watch yourself. No need for anyone else to die."

His warning left a lump in my throat, and I clunked back to stand beside Sile again without answering. He was frowning at me like he was waiting for an explanation. "A family friend," I told him as vaguely as I knew how.

Sile didn't ask anything about it. He just grabbed my shoulder to keep me from running off again, and steered me directly toward the second armory building. I had a new saddle waiting for me there.

Getting Mavrik into the saddle was a spectacle. We

even had an audience. A few other riders and students started to gather around to watch me trying to put a saddle on my wild dragon.

It wasn't a very big saddle, because I wasn't a very big person, and I could carry it fairly easily. But when Mavrik saw it, he hissed at me where he was crouched on his belly. He made angry chattering noises, swishing his long tail, and tracking my movements with his bright yellow eyes as I lugged the saddle over toward him.

"Come on, it's not that bad." I grumbled.

He snorted, sending a blast of hot air into my face. A few of the spectators laughed.

"I don't like it any more than you do. Let's just get it over with." I slung the saddle over my shoulder, lifting it up as high as I could to sling it over his neck. Mavrik growled lowly, snorted again, and narrowed his eyes angrily.

Sile stepped in to help me get the hard, shaped bottom of the saddle fitted onto the grooves and horns of Mavrik's back. It fit like a glove, and he quickly walked me through a blurred lesson in strapping the saddle into place. A pair of very thick leather belts went around his neck and under his wing arms. Lesser straps stabilized it, running under his belly to keep the saddle from sliding around.

Once we'd finished, Sile pulled me back quickly as

Mavrik rose up and shook himself. The saddle stayed put, fixed to his back between his neck and wing arms. He snarled at it, twisting around like he didn't approve, and finally cutting an accusing glare right at me.

I threw my hands up in surrender. "It's not my fault! I can't just cling to you and hope you don't drop me."

The dragon licked his chops, and slicked his ears back like an angry cat as he hunkered down again.

"Time for a test drive." Sile was smirking from ear to ear.

My stomach fell, and as he helped me up into the saddle, I was already feeling sick. He showed me how to fit my legs down into the pair of deep, boot-like sheaths crafted into the sides of the saddle. They came up to my knees, and were so snug it was like wearing a second pair of extra tall boots.

"How's the fit? Can you move your feet?" Sile asked.

I shook my head. "No, not much."

"Good." He started rattling off instructions, making me queasy as I tried not to think about what I was about to do. "This is primarily what anchors you into the saddle. Here, you see these handles are like the ones on my saddle. During take off and high-intensity maneuvers, you're going to have to lean into his speed and hold on. The gauntlets you're wearing are meant to help you keep a grip. That's why the palms are coated with resin. Don't fight against his speed. Move with it. If you resist, you're going to get slung all over the place. It's like any relationship, if you go into it unwilling to move and think as one, it can only end in disaster."

"How do I steer?" I was beginning to panic. I could tell my brief lesson in the basics of flying was almost over. Mavrik was beginning to shift around anxiously again.

Sile grabbed my hand, showing me how to grip the polished bone handles. They were positioned on what looked like a circular pieces of metal, about the size of a dinner plate, built into the sides of the saddle. I'd assumed they were just to keep the handle from coming unstitched, but Sile twisted my hand and showed me that the round metal pieces actually rotated if you pushed hard enough.

"Left and right." he told me in a hurried voice. "When you twist them, it puts a small amount of pressure against his side. He can feel it, and knows which way you want him to go. You'll have to work with him to get used to it. Remember, he's never flown with anyone, either. You have to teach each other. You'll come up with your own signals and body language to communicate in the air."

I was about to ask how to tell him to land, but Sile was gone in a flash. He jogged backwards away from us as Mavrik began to stand, making me bob around in the saddle as I gripped the handles for dear life. I squinted my eyes shut, clinging with all my might as I felt the dragon shake himself again. He was still writhing around, snarling about the strange feeling of the saddle on his back. All I could do was hang on and pray he wasn't going to kill me.

Right away, the feel of Mavrik's flight was completely different from anything I'd experienced with Sile. When he leapt into the sky, I could feel the force and power of his body working around me as he pumped his wings. I heard him roar, felt his sides swelling and shrinking against my legs as he breathed, and watched the earth fall away. The crowd of spectators became like little dark spots far below.

When Mavrik took off, it wasn't chaos. I didn't feel like I was going to get flung off his back. I felt anchored, and almost as though I was a part of him. It felt right, and it gave me such a rush of excitement that I couldn't help but scream out. He stretched his wings wide, leveling off and letting out another belting cry of his own. He flicked a look back at me, as though making sure I was still attached to him. I was grinning like an idiot, laughing as I held on for dear life.

Suddenly there was another trumpeting roar directly to my right. It was so loud, and seemingly out of nowhere, that it startled me. I looked over, and couldn't believe it. Felix and Nova were flying upside down right next to me, so close I could have reached out and grabbed his helmet if I wanted. He waved at me. I could hear him laughing, too, even over the rush of the wind.

Just as quickly as he'd appeared, I watched him dive away. Nova spun into a tight roll, swirling down toward the ground. Before I could think about the intensity of a move like that … Mavrik decided to take up the chase. He snapped his wings in tight against his sides, and immediately we plummeted downward. I screamed because there was nothing else I could do other than hang on.

We chased Nova like two eagles playing tag, darting through the sky. We did dives, we rolled, we flew up until we breached the clouds and saw nothing but endless sky above.

Nova really was a big female. She was way bigger than Mavrik, with golden and brown markings on her scales like a jungle snake. She was bigger, but Mavrik was faster. When he switched on the speed, there was no catching us, and we dove through the clouds like a charge of blue lightning.

It was indescribable, and right away I knew it was the greatest rush I'd ever experience. I also knew I'd never get enough of it. If being a dragonrider meant I got to do this every day, I'd jog as many laps and memorize as many maps as I had to. I wasn't going to give this up—not ever.

eight

"We're going to be the best," Felix declared as we lay awake in our beds. After a day like that, neither of us could sleep. My heart was still racing, and I couldn't stop grinning. All I could think about was flying again, and how soon I'd be allowed back in the saddle.

"Trust me, I know. I can feel it. We're going to be the best riders this academy has ever seen," he went on.

I laughed. "We haven't even had our first real lesson yet, Felix," I reminded him.

He didn't seem to think that was a problem. He went on and on, talking about our bright future, until he finally fell asleep. As soon as I heard him start to snore, I got up and put my boots back on as quietly as I could.

The craftsmen were going to be leaving tomorrow. All the saddles and armor had been finished, and so they would go back to their homes and private workshops. Mr. Crookin would go with them, and I had to get Katty's letter into his saddlebag before he left.

I crept out of the dormitory and into the night. The academy was quiet, and every building was dark except for a few rooms in the instructors' dormitory. I slipped through the shadows, and was out of breath by the time I reached the smithing armory. All of Mr. Crookin's gear was still there, packed up and ready to move out in the morning.

I took Katty's letter, folded it up the way Felix had shown me, and tucked it carefully into one of his saddlebags. With a big sigh of relief, I stood up and started back for my room. Thousands of stars twinkled overhead, and the moonlight made long, ghostly shadows on the ground.

I'd just reached the edge of the tackmasters' armory, keeping out of sight as much as possible in case there were any instructors still awake, when the sound of two voices made me freeze in place.

A cold shiver of fear ran down my spine. The voices were coming closer. I sucked in a sharp breath, and ducked into the nearest workstation that was still crowded with equipment. Hiding behind a big wooden crate, I waited.

The voices kept coming closer, and I could hear the crunch of footsteps. I recognized one of the voices right away; it was Lyon Cromwell. But I didn't recognize the other one. It sounded like a much older man, maybe even an instructor.

"You're absolutely sure about that? Every morning?" the man's voice asked in a snapping tone.

"Oh yeah, we've all seen them," Lyon was quick to answer. "Trust me. He's up there before the call to arms, running drills with both of them like clockwork. He's giving them all the lessons a week ahead of time, so tomorrow they should start aerial maneuvers."

The unknown man made a thoughtful, growling noise. "We hadn't anticipated on the halfbreed, but I suppose it won't be a problem. Fledglings wouldn't know how to respond to such an ... unforeseen accident."

"Oh, I wouldn't worry about that little rat," Lyon scoffed. "He won't last a week in real training. It's a joke they've even let him stay here this long."

The man didn't sound so sure. "Lieutenant Derrick is not an idiot. If you had half a brain yourself, you'd realize that. He's up to something. Our best chance is to act now, before any plan he's cooking up has had time to be fully realized."

"Right." Lyon didn't sound too happy about being called dumb, but he didn't argue. "Well, I held up my end, so I expect you to hold up yours."

It was the older man's turn to scoff. "Watch your mouth, boy, and remember your place. You will be compensated, as long as everything goes according to plan."

I ducked down, and tried to make myself into the smallest ball I possibly could when their footsteps went past. Their voices started to get faint then, and they moved away toward the Roost. After a few minutes, I couldn't hear them at all anymore.

At first, I was too afraid to even think of moving. I couldn't believe what I'd heard. Lyon was planning something bad, and it sounded like it was going to be aimed at Sile. I was so terrified of being caught out here alone, where no one would hear me scream for help, but I couldn't stay in the armory all night. So I waited a few more minutes, until I was absolutely sure they weren't coming back, and started for the student dormitory in a sprint.

I didn't stop or look back until I'd slammed the bedroom door shut behind me. There wasn't a lock on it, so I just stood with my back against it, gasping for breath. My heart was pumping like mad, and I was numb from head to toe.

Felix bolted upright as soon as the door slammed, and he glared at me sleepily with his hair ruffled up like a messy haystack. "What's the big idea? You scared me to death!" He growled as he grabbed his blanket and rolled back over.

"F-Felix!" I could barely get the words out because of how hard I was breathing. "Outside, I heard someone talking to Lyon! Tomorrow morning, when we fly, Sile is—!"

"—probably gonna kick your butt for staying up too late," he interrupted angrily. "Would you go to sleep already? And quit slamming the door. You scared me to death."

"But I heard—!" I tried to spit the words out before I ran out of breath.

"Right now all I can hear is you keeping me awake!" Felix growled again, grabbing his pillow and covering his head with it. That was the end of the conversation.

I sat down on the edge of my bed and tried to think. There had to be some logical explanation for what I'd heard; something that wasn't as bad as how it had sounded. But no matter what I came up with, I was still left with a swirling sense of doom in the pit of my stomach.

Something bad was going to happen, and I was the only one who knew.

nine

It was hard to get excited about my first day of training when I had a big black cloud of worry hanging over my head. I got up before Felix did, got dressed, and waited on him to catch up so we could meet Sile before the call to arms. We had patterns to learn and laps to run before our day officially began.

"What's with you?" Felix asked me on the way to the Roost. "You look like you've seen a ghost."

I shot him a glare. "I tried to tell you last night. I heard Lyon talking to someone. He's plotting against Sile."

"Pfft!" Felix slapped my shoulder teasingly. "You're just paranoid. Sile is one of the most decorated instructors here. Why would anyone want to plot against him?"

I didn't know. All I knew is what I'd heard, and it hadn't sounded like they were planning a surprise party for him.

Sile was waiting for us. He was already saddled up and ready to fly, standing in his full armor like he had been the first day I saw him at Ulric's house. He coached us hurriedly through putting on our own saddles again, and then we were off.

The sun was just beginning to rise over the eastern mountains, making the sky a deep purplish red. The air was cold, and my teeth chattered under my helmet as I watched Sile and Felix surge forward into the sky on either side of me. We gained speed and altitude, leaving the dark ground behind and charging toward the sunrise.

Mavrik seemed to be able to sense my apprehension. He kept flicking his big yellow eyes back at me, making curious chittering noises as he chased Valla and Nova through the air. I kept my eyes on Sile, watching as he took the lead and began to give us signals to follow him in a V-shaped pattern.

I could see him clearly off my left wing, and he started to guide us through a long sweeping pattern that took us around the outermost perimeter of the valley. We did steep climbs, steeper dives, and sharp banking turns.

I was beginning to think Felix was right. Maybe I was

just being paranoid, and I'd just misunderstood what I'd heard last night. There really was nothing to be worried about at all.

Then Sile gave the signal to do a barrel roll.

I watched him veer to the right, toward me, and begin another steep descent. Valla drew her wings in, and they began to roll downwards into a layer of clouds. Out of the corner of my eye, I saw Felix start to follow, mimicking Sile's movements.

Suddenly, something snapped.

It made such a loud crack I could hear it even over the rush of the wind that hummed past my helmet. I ducked just in time as a piece of metal went flying past my head so fast it probably would have knocked me out cold. I looked back over my shoulder, trying to figure out what it was. I was almost sure it looked like a buckle.

Valla let out a high-pitched shriek that sounded like pure panic. Mavrik answered her with a thrumming roar, and before I could think, he snapped his wings in tight and started to dive after her. All I could do was hang on, searching frantically for some sign of Valla, or even Felix, as we dove through the clouds. We streaked downwards, and I couldn't see anything except the occasional blur of ground through the haze.

Then I saw her. Valla flared her white wings right below us, catching the air and coming to a sudden halt.

I yelled at the top of my lungs. We were going to hit her!

Mavrik put on more speed, making a sharp twist so that we just barely missed her as we blitzed down through the air. A second later, and we would have struck her head-on. I caught a glimpse of Valla as we blurred past; she wasn't wearing a saddle anymore. My heart stopped, I looked frantically through the clouds below, searching for Sile.

He was in freefall, lost somewhere in the haze.

We hadn't been trained to handle something like this yet. I couldn't hear anything but the rush of wind, couldn't see anything but the clouds all around us, but I could sense the ground was growing closer and closer with each passing second. If I couldn't find him in time, if he hit the ground from this high up ...

Then I saw him.

Sile was falling through the air like a stone. His helmet was missing, and I could see his mouth was open like he was screaming as he flailed through the air. He saw me in that same instant. Our eyes met, and I knew I was about to watch him die unless I did something.

I leaned down against Mavrik's back, squeezing the saddle handles and giving the signal for him to fly faster. The ground was getting closer. I could see it rushing up to meet us. Mavrik rolled to avoid cliffs as we glanced near the sides of the mountains.

Just a few feet away from Sile, I reached my hand out toward him. He was clawing at the air, trying to grab onto me. I couldn't reach him. My arms were just a few inches too short. I tried to lean out further, and still keep a grip on my own saddle. My fingertips brushed his. I saw the panic, the sheer terror in his eyes.

Something came over me like a flood of eerie calm. Everything got quiet in my mind. Fear melted away. I let go of the saddle completely, anchored to it only with my feet in the sheaths, and lunged out toward him. I grabbed Sile by the front of his breastplate, and he clung to me as I dragged him in toward the saddle.

Sile just barely got his fingers hooked onto my saddle before we were jerked violently backwards. Mavrik flared his wings to put on the brakes, stretching out his hind legs and kicking off the ground just in time. He leapt back into the air, and I felt my heart jump into the back of my throat as the ground fell away again.

When we landed safely back at the academy, I was shaking so badly I couldn't even get out of the saddle at first. Felix landed nearby, and he was yelling and waving his arms as he ran toward us. Sile climbed down from where he'd been piggybacking on my saddle, and he looked shaken, too. He was cradling one of his arms against his body like he'd been hurt.

I pulled off my helmet, taking a few deep breaths

and trying to calm down. But I was still trembling all over, and feeling lightheaded like I might pass out. When I tried climbing down from the saddle, I got my foot stuck and I fell flat onto my back, looking up into the early morning sky. Mavrik's big head appeared over me, sniffing and pressing his scaled nose against my chest.

"Good job," I told him breathlessly, patting his snout.

Felix was frantic as he rushed over to haul me back up to my feet. "What happened?!"

I shook my head. "I'm not sure. I think something happened to his saddle."

When I looked up to find Sile and ask him, he was walking away. An audience of other students and instructors was gathering around us. Someone had sounded the alarm when Valla had landed without a saddle or rider on her back.

Sile was staggering away from us, and his face looked pasty. He leaned on one of the other instructors and hobbled away through the crowd. He didn't even look back.

Felix was looking me over like he was searching for damage. "How is that possible? I've never heard of that happening before. Someone would have to intentionally compromise it for it to just break like tha—" he stopped short, and gave me a wide-eyed look.

I glared at him darkly. "Still think I'm just paranoid?"

Felix didn't answer. He didn't have to. I could see on his face that this was bad. Someone had just tried to kill Sile Derrick by breaking his saddle on purpose. They'd tried to do it and make it look like a terrible accident.

The instructors still standing around began shouting at us to move along, to get back to our routine. Gradually, everyone began to disperse. Felix gave me a little shove with his elbow, and I knew we had to get back to our own schedule. Sile wouldn't want us slacking off, even if he was hurt.

It took us longer to run our laps while dressed in full armor, but since our flight had been cut short, we still made it to the breaking dome before the call to arms sounded. All the other students in the academy flooded in, almost a hundred total. The older classes looked more distinguished, more like men or proud warriors, and they glared at me like there was a diseased mouse in their midst when we came inside.

I stayed close to Felix, following him to stand at the front of the group with the other first-year fledglings. Academy Commander Rayken was talking with a few of the other high-ranking instructors in full battle armor, whispering to each other in low voices before they finally turned to the crowd of waiting students. The dome became silent, and we all watched as Rayken stepped forward to address us.

"I'm sure you've all heard about Lieutenant Derrick's unfortunate accident this morning," the commander spoke loudly. "You'll be relieved to hear that his injuries were minor, and he will be back in service tomorrow. Let this be a lesson to all of you. Check your gear each and every time you ride. Never assume anything, and be prepared for everything."

I swallowed stiffly, and was glad he hadn't said anything about my involvement. I had a pretty good idea that people would look at me more as a culprit than a hero.

The commander waved a hand then, dismissing that topic with no more ceremony. "Back to business. Allow me to welcome you to Blybrig Academy. For some of you, this is your first time to stand in our midst. For others, you are already a part of our brotherhood."

He went on, talking about the proud history of the dragonriders and our place as the pride of the king's forces. It was inspiring to look around and see the other, older young men standing around me. We all wore the same style of uniform, tunics and black pants. But we fledglings all wore navy blue tunics with the golden eagle, while the second year students wore black tunics with blue stripes down the arms and sides. They also wore long navy blue cloaks pinned around their shoulders by a golden clasp shaped like the king's eagle. It made them look way more professional and polished than we did.

The older students also had a hardened ferocity in their eyes, and they stood stiffly at attention with their hands clasped behind their backs. I still didn't see how I would ever fit in with these guys. I felt like a fox that'd been lined up with the hunting hounds. Sooner or later, someone was going to sound the horn and I would have to run for my life.

The Academy Commander dismissed us with a salute, clasping a fist over his breastplate that all the older students returned with a shout. Then we started to break up into our respective classes. The older students left first, dispersing outside to go about their schedules, and the rest of us in the fledgling class started to flock to the gymnasium for our first round of combat training.

The gymnasium was just a big, open building with a dirt floor. It was lit with bulky iron chandeliers that had thick candles burning, making the place feel like some kind of dungeon. There were practice dummies made out of straw lined up against the far walls, and several large chalk circles drawn out on the floor for sparring.

The instructor in charge of teaching us combat was another lieutenant named Morrig. He wasn't an especially large or burly man, but he had that same coldness in his eyes that made me immediately afraid of him. He gave us all blunt practice swords, and broke us up into groups of two. I made sure to partner with Felix. There were thirteen of us in all, so he pulled one student aside to be his partner while he showed us how to move through each maneuver.

We started with simple parries and strikes, and ran through drills taking turns being offensive and defensive until everyone was exhausted. Then we moved on to hand-to-hand sparring.

I had been dreading this from the beginning. I was so much smaller than everyone else; I knew I didn't stand a chance in a wrestling match. Thankfully, today was just for instruction, for learning the different ways to pin someone, or disable an enemy that was armed with a sword.

Felix was really good at it. He was one of the tallest of the boys, and he was incredibly strong. So naturally, he pinned me every time, and I wound up with a face full of dirt. He wasn't going easy on me just because of my size.

Morrig ran us through drill after drill, move after move, and ended the first day of combat training by having us do pushups, sit-ups, and spend nearly an hour lifting big iron weights. When we finished, everyone was absolutely filthy and none of us even had the energy to look one another in the eye.

By the time we got to the dining hall, I'd forgotten all about Sile's accident that morning. All I could think about was lunch. Felix brought us a tray of food to share, and I started stuffing my face before he even sat down.

"So, you're sure it was Lyon you heard last night?" Felix asked suddenly. I couldn't help but notice how nervous he looked.

I nodded. "I'm sure."

"The instructors are writing this off as an accident. But I've been thinking about it, and there's just no way it could have been. You've seen our saddles. You'd have to intentionally cut the straps for one to fall off like that." Felix leaned in to whisper. "Tonight, when we're done with academics, we're going to go looking for his saddle. It's got to be just lying in the dirt out there. I want to see if the straps really were cut."

I swallowed my mouthful of food. "What if we get caught? That's a long way to walk."

Felix shook his head. "I'm not saying we walk. We fly out there, check it out, and come back. It's the only way to be sure."

I wasn't sold on the idea. But then, I'd heard Lyon plotting first hand. I knew what I heard, and there was no question in my mind that someone had done something to Sile's saddle to make him fall like that. But once Felix got an idea in his head, there was no way to talk him out of it. I was beginning to realize that was a trend with him.

After lunch, we had our first official lesson in flying.

We were taught how to properly put on our saddles, piece by piece, which buckle went where, and how the fit should be. After going to so much trouble, I started to realize why Felix was so baffled at the way Sile's saddle had fallen off. Someone really would have to intentionally damage a saddle in a big way to make it come off like that.

The instructor checked all our saddles twice over, making doubly sure they were put on properly before we took to the air and began learning basic patterns. Felix and I had already gone over this basic stuff a few times with Sile, so we knew what to do. For the first time, I felt a little bit confident.

After flight training, we began our studies in academics and cartography. That lasted the rest of the afternoon, and we were dismissed for the day as the sun started to set. Of course, we were expected to study and practice everything we'd learned that day, but all I wanted was a bath and something to eat.

When I finally flopped down onto my bed, I tried not to think about how every muscle in my body ached. I thought it was safe to steal a few minutes of sleep before I tried studying my maps again. Then the door opened, and a shoe hit me in the face.

"Hey, what're you doing?" Felix laughed, armed with his second shoe in case the first one didn't wake me up.

"We've still got to study, you know."

I groaned, and rolled onto my back. I was prepared to take his other boot to the head if it meant I could sleep for even fifteen minutes. "I'm exhausted. I can't feel my legs."

"Oh come on, don't be a baby." He teased. "We need to at least look busy. As soon as evening roll call is over, and everything gets really quiet, we're going to find that saddle."

He had gone over his plan with me about thirty times already. I still wasn't so sure this was going to work. I hadn't paid much attention to where we were exactly when I'd caught Sile in the air, much less where his saddle had landed. However, I did have a pretty good idea of what would happen if we got caught.

"It was incredible. You know, the way you caught him like that," he said suddenly.

I rolled my head over to see if he was making fun of me or not. He wasn't. His face looked serious, if not a little proud. "I couldn't just let him fall like that. Besides, I'm pretty sure none of the other instructors would want to take me on as a student. If he dies, that's the end of my career."

Felix laughed a little. "Yeah, good point."

I only snoozed for a half hour or so before guilt forced me to study. Felix and I sat up by candlelight, studying our maps, and going through the complex language of hand-signals we'd only just begun to learn. Right after the evening horn blew, we started hearing the sounds of talking and footsteps outside as the various sponsors checked their student's rooms to be sure everyone was accounted for.

Sile knocked on our door, and I got a hard lump in the back of my throat when I saw him standing in the doorway. He had one arm in a sling, and a bandage on one side of his neck. He looked between us as we sat on our individual beds, our maps spread out in front of us.

"How was it?" Sile asked. I noticed he was making an effort not to look me in the eye.

"Not bad," Felix piped up. "I've got some questions about a few of the parry moves, but I figured I would just wait and see if we could go through them tomorrow morning before combat training. How's the arm?"

Sile sighed and shook his head a little. "It's just a precaution. The infirmary insisted I wear it for at least one day. Knocked out of socket, they said. No real harm done." He looked at me then, and I felt like I'd been nailed to a wall. "Jae, I need to talk to you."

I swallowed hard. "Yes sir."

Felix cast me a haunted look as I got off my bed, stepped into my boots, and followed Sile out into the hallway.

We were alone outside the closed door of my dorm room, and Sile stood with his side to me for a moment as though he were collecting his thoughts. I had no idea what he was going to say, but before he got a word out, my mouth ran away with me.

"Lieutenant Derrick, I think someone is trying to kill you," I blurted.

He turned a perplexed expression down at me. "Because of what happened today?"

"Well, yes, but there's something else." My face got hot, and I dropped my gaze down to the tops of my boots. "I was out at the armories last night, I wanted to send a letter back home with one of the craftsmen, and I heard someone else out there. They were talking about us, and it sounded like they were going to do something bad."

His expression became intensely serious. "Who? Did you see them? Did you recognize who it was?"

I choked. I had recognized Lyon's voice, of course. But I hadn't seen him. I hadn't actually seen anyone. I didn't want to run the risk of pointing a finger at the wrong person, so I just shook my head. "No, it was really dark. I couldn't see who it was. I mentioned it to Felix, and he said I was just being paranoid. I really thought maybe he was right. I didn't want to assume anything. I'm sorry, sir. I should have said something."

Sile let out a loud, noisy sigh. I wasn't sure what he'd

do or say to that. I almost expected to get struck for not speaking up sooner. Instead, I felt a heavy hand fall on my shoulder.

He was smiling down at me, and I could have sworn his eyes seemed almost sad. "Jae, you saved my life today. What you did was stupid, but incredibly brave. Thank you."

I hesitated. "Sir, is someone trying to kill you?"

His expression twitched. I saw darkness in his eyes, and that sense of doom burrowed into the pit of my gut. It made me nauseated.

"Apparently so," he answered. He didn't sound surprised at all.

ten

Felix was eager to get out and find the remains of Sile's broken saddle. He still wanted hard evidence. As soon as the academy was silent, and anyone with any sense was resting up for the next day, he dragged me out of bed and out the door. I was nervous about it; we weren't allowed to be out of our rooms like this, much less flying without an instructor's permission. If something went wrong, no one would even realize we were gone until tomorrow morning.

But Felix wasn't backing down. He had decided we would take his dragon and ride together. She was big enough to carry both of us without any problems, and it would be easier to sneak one dragon out instead of two. I was just anxious to get this over with. The sooner he got his proof, the sooner I could sleep.

Standing outside the Roost, I kept a lookout while he went inside to saddle her up. I didn't like standing out there alone in the open. Somehow, I had the feeling that if we did get caught, I'd be the one who got blamed for this regardless of anything Felix said. I was the bad influence, after all. I was the halfbreed.

The night air was quiet and the wind was still. Looking up, the stars were so bright they made the whole horizon glitter. There was plenty of light to see by, so I started to hope that maybe we would actually find the lost remains of Sile's saddle.

I heard a rustling behind me, and let out a sigh of relief. I just assumed it was Felix coming back with his dragon.

But it wasn't. Not even close.

I turned around right into an oncoming fist. Someone hit me so hard across my face that it sent me stumbling backwards. My vision blurred. My nose stung. I could taste blood coming from my nose and mouth.

"You just keep getting in my way." I couldn't see who hit me, but I heard Lyon's voice laughing over me. I knew it was him. "You really should've just taken the hint and quit while you were ahead. Now you're in my way again."

There was more laughter coming from some other guys standing behind them. My vision cleared enough that I could see them under the starlight. Four older boys, including Lyon, were circling me. They were all fledglings from my class—Lyon's friends.

I scrambled to get back up, but Lyon was quicker. Just as soon as I'd gotten my feet under me, he hit me again in the stomach so hard I fell forward. I was gasping and wheezing for breath, crawling across the ground to get away.

"No one wants you here. You'll never be one of us. Don't you get that?" He snarled over me, and grabbed a fistful of my hair to jerk my head back so I had to look at him in the eye. "You will never be worth anything to anyone. You think Felix cares about you? He doesn't. No one cares anything about halfbreeds. You're nothing but filth, and that's all you'll ever be."

The other three boys circled me again, and one reared back to kick me in the ribs. I couldn't catch my breath to even cry out for help. It might take half an hour for Felix to get his saddle ready, if he did it the way he was supposed to, and by then ... I wasn't sure how much of me would be left.

They were kicking me, hitting me as hard as they could. One of them had come armed with his riding gauntlets, and when he hit me, it was like being smacked with solid iron. I curled into a ball, covering my head with my arms, and prayed for it to end.

Suddenly, it stopped.

I was afraid to look up and see why. I was afraid maybe one of them had come with a sword, or gone to get some other weapon to finish me off. But what I heard was the sound of fighting, of frantic shouting, and punches being swung.

When I finally looked up, I saw Felix standing over me with his hands balled into fists. He had a crazed look of rage on his face, and his lips were curled up into a snarl. One of the other boys was already lying unconscious nearby.

"Get up, Jae." Felix growled down at me. "I can't take them all by myself."

I was in pain from the hits I'd already taken. But at that moment, it didn't matter. I got up. Felix was fighting for me, and I wasn't going to let him do it alone. I put up my fists, facing the three boys left standing. Lyon was one of them, and he looked like he wanted to kill me. He dove at me first.

And then it was a brawl.

Even if I wasn't a good fighter, I could at least watch Felix's back. He hit them so hard it made me cringe. He was a pretty big guy already, bigger than Lyon, and twice as strong. I saw so much pent up anger in the way he fought them, and even when he took hits, he never quit. At least, not until he had his boot on Lyon's face and was grinding it into the dust.

"Come after him again, and I'll break both your arms," Felix promised with a snarl. "Not even your parents will be able to recognize what's left of you."

When Lyon managed to worm his way out from under Felix's heel, he immediately started to run, and the rest of the boys went with him. They disappeared into the night, and left their unconscious friend just lying there.

I couldn't believe it was over. I was afraid to relax, expecting another attack to come out of nowhere. But they didn't come back. The night was just as quiet as it had been before.

I stood beside Felix, blood dripping from my nose down the front of my nightshirt, and didn't dare let my guard down until I saw him drop his arms. We were both breathing hard, spattered with blood, and looking at each other with no idea what to say.

At last, Felix's shoulders sagged and he came over to grab my chin, jerking my face up to poke at my bloody nose.

I winced and tried to squirm away. "Stop it! I'm fine!" I didn't like they way he hovered over me like some kind of a worried parent. It was humiliating to be treated like a little kid, and I was already embarrassed that he'd had to save me in the first place.

"You're lucky it's not broken," he reminded me as he let me go.

I staggered back, still panting as I glared defiantly up at him. "Why do you keep doing that? Why do you care what happens to me? No one else does!"

Lyon's venomous words were still ringing in my ears, reminding me of the cold truths I feared the most. I didn't know why Felix was being so nice to me. I didn't want to suspect that he was just toying with me. But I couldn't help it. No one else wanted to be a friend to me, especially none of the other fledglings.

"You think I should just let them kill you?" He yelled back. "Just because of who your mother was?"

I fought to choke back the tears that stung in my eyes. "Anyone else would! So why? Why do you keep doing this? I deserve to know!"

He looked at me like it was the stupidest question in the world. I heard him curse under his breath. "You'd do the same for me, wouldn't you?"

I stared at him. He'd answered my dumb question with another dumb question. "Yes."

He pointed at me accusingly. "That's why. You understand that this isn't just a contest to see who can be better between you and me, who can outrank the other, or screw the other over behind their back. Just because your mother is a gray elf doesn't make your life any less valuable than mine. I know you'd sacrifice just as much if it were my face being kicked into the dirt. Am I right? So you tell me, why would I stick my neck out for someone like that? Why would I want someone like that as my friend?"

I couldn't answer him. I just stared at him, unable to keep tears from streaming down my face. He stomped toward me, grabbing the back of my shirt and giving me a shove back toward the dormitory.

"Come on, we've gotta get back inside before someone sees us. Forget about the stupid saddle." He growled through clenched teeth as he kept me moving onward.

I knew he was angry. Even if I wasn't sure why, I still felt like it was my fault. After cleaning my face up, pinching my nose to stop the bleeding, and assessing the damage to the rest of my body, I curled into my bed. Except for some bad bruises, I'd gotten away without any serious injuries.

Felix was awake, still looking like he was fuming with rage where he sat in his own bed. As soon as I was settled, lying with my back to him, he doused the candle and the room went dark.

"Felix?" I asked, not really expecting him to answer. "What?"

I squeezed my eyes shut. "Thank you."

He was quiet for a moment, and then I heard him make a loud, exasperated sigh. "You're welcome."

eleven

As the weeks passed, every morning started early, with us flying drills as usual. Then we ran our laps, and Felix always ended up practically pushing me like a wheelbarrow so I didn't collapse. Then combat training lasted the rest of the morning, and I was essentially Felix's practice dummy. He never slacked off, never went easy on me, but always apologized whenever he nearly choked me unconscious or gave me a new horrific-looking bruise. I knew he was trying to help me. No one else was going to go easy on me, and he wouldn't be doing me any favors if he did.

I had been hoping I'd get tougher, or stronger, but it felt like I was actually getting worse. My parries weren't right. My strikes were too slow and weak. Watching me try to wrestle and pin Felix, who was twice my size, probably looked like a chicken trying to pin an angry bull. The instructors yelled until it bored into my ears, telling me to be faster, to work harder, and to quit being an embarrassment to the academy.

In the air, however, I wasn't an embarrassment. Even the instructors had to give me some credit for that. Maybe I couldn't pin Felix on the ground, but in the air it was a whole different story. Mavrik was fast, aggressive, and he could outmaneuver anyone. It was like he wasn't even aware I was on his back. Sile was right; we did form our own little language of body signals and touches to communicate while we flew. Mavrik was smart, and he seemed to understand me better and better each day. We became two parts of the same powerful entity.

I was also good at memorizing the maps. I had mine down like the back of my hand in two weeks flat. I never missed a mark or a single detail, and I even coached Felix some because he struggled with it a lot more than I did.

Things weren't going great, but they weren't going as badly as they could have been. After our showdown that night at the Roost, Lyon stayed away from me. He shot us poisonous looks from afar, but pretty much kept his distance. Felix had hit him hard enough to make an impression, apparently.

The days were so blurred together, with every hour either filled with some kind of training, studying, or sleeping, that I totally lost track of time. I didn't hear anything else about a plot against Sile. There were no more malfunctioning saddles, or aerial rescues. Things fell into a predictable, constant routine that gave me a sense of comfort and stability I'd never had before. For the first time, I had a plan. I had something to do, somewhere I had to be, and responsibilities.

Our combat training became more intense, and more specific to weapons we were better suited to use. Lieutenant Morrig wasn't sure what to do with me. My arm wasn't long enough for a short sword. I wasn't tall enough for a spear. I wasn't strong enough for an axe or a mace. He was puzzled, and so I just kept switching weapons, hoping one would eventually be the right fit.

We also learned archery, and the academics shifted from memorizing maps and hand signs, to learning about the native plants and animals of Luntharda. They made it sound so horrifying, and described huge bloodthirsty beasts, poisonous streams, and even carnivorous trees. Secretly, I found it all really interesting. My mother had always told me stories about the forest, but never in such detail.

We also learned how about how to treat wounds in the field. We learned to set broken bones, to make poultices and salves from various plants to stave off infection, and how to stitch up gashes and cuts. I was pretty good at it because my fingers were smaller, and I'd seen so much of my own blood that being around wounds didn't make me queasy like it did some of the others.

Summer made the valley incredibly hot during the day. It baked the earth like clay in a kiln, and made all the plants and grass shrivel up. At night it was pretty cool, so we usually stayed inside and studied. None of us had the energy left at the end of the day to risk getting caught out on the grounds anyway.

I wasn't aware how much time had passed, or even what month it was, until Felix started jabbering about the officer's ball. Apparently, once a year, every officer of note was invited to a grand ball held at a certain noble's home. The rich families of Maldobar argued over who should host it since it was, according to Felix, the best place to go shopping for a potential spouse. It was a status symbol because sometimes the king attended. There'd be wine, dancing, music, food, and pretty girls as far as the eye could see. Felix was absolutely giddy about it.

"We aren't officers yet," I reminded him as we sat at the dinner table. I had my face in a dusty old book, reading about the carnivorous trees that grew in Luntharda. "What makes you think we'll get to have any fun?"

"We will, we just won't be allowed to dance or talk

with any of the girls," Felix countered. "We can look, but we aren't supposed to approach."

A few of the other fledgling students sitting around us nodded in agreement. Since our confrontation with Lyon, little by little, I'd started to earn the tiniest amount of acceptance from my peers. I wasn't dumb enough to think they liked me, but they were willing to tolerate me now. I guess they'd figured out that if they couldn't get rid of me, they might as well get used to me being around.

"So, what you mean by that is you're going to do it anyway?" I peered over the top of my book at him.

Felix was grinning from ear to ear. "Of course. It's only punishable if you get caught."

I rolled my eyes. "I don't see what the big deal is. It's just a bunch of silly, giggling girls. What's so interesting about them?"

Felix smacked my book out of my hands down onto the table. "Are you crazy? Don't you have a girl back home?"

I glared at him. I'd made the mistake of telling him about Katty when this all started. I'd even let him talk me into sending her a letter. But I hadn't received any reply at all from her. I didn't know if she'd even gotten my letter in the first place.

"No." I grumbled, crossing my arms over my chest. "I told you, she's just my friend."

"It starts with friends," Felix was grinning cattishly again, and a few of the other students around him had joined in. "Then you go in for the kiss."

"You sound like an idiot, you know." I arched a brow at him. "Even if you did find some way to sneak off and talk to a girl, you're not an officer yet. None of us are. We're just students. And aren't we supposed to be serving food and manning the doors and carriages? What girl is going to want to talk to a glorified butler?"

Felix wasn't listening anymore. He'd started snickering and talking to someone else who appreciated the topic of girls more than I did. I wasn't going to let myself get caught up in any kind of grand vision of how the ball would be. It would be interesting to be in a noble's home, watch the couples dance, and see how the rich and glamorous got to live. But I was sure I'd get stared at worse than usual. What noble wanted a dirty halfbreed in their house?

We finished dinner and dispersed to our rooms. I took my time bathing. When I came back our room, Felix was stretched out on his bed studying.

"You got something today," he said, pointing to my bed on the other side of the room.

There was a small square envelope sitting on my bed with my name, Jaevid Broadfeather, written on the outside. I was bewildered. We were more than halfway through the training year, and no one had sent me anything before. I went over and picked it up, tearing it open carefully to unfold the paper tucked inside.

"It's from your girl, isn't it?" Felix was standing right over me, breathing down my neck. "I want to see. C'mon you owe me, especially after I helped you write the first one."

I didn't want to share it. I tried to turn so he couldn't see it, holding it down and away. Before I could read a single word, he snatched it out of my hands and darted away. I chased him, trying to grab it back while he laughed. He held it high over his head and started reading it out loud.

"Stop it, Felix!" I yelled, jumping to try and grab it. "Give it back!"

"Ooh look, she says she misses you. She even drew a little heart there for you at the bottom of the page." He teased, finally let me have the letter back. I gave him a good punch in the arm before I retreated back to my bed and started reading it.

I didn't interpret anything in Katty's letter as even remotely out of the ordinary, much less romantic. And there definitely wasn't a heart drawn at the bottom of the page. She wrote that she was glad I was doing well, and proud that I'd made it into the dragonrider's academy. She was looking forward to seeing me when I got to come home between training years, and said that she missed me. Her father had started teaching her blacksmithing full time now, and had even given her the official title of his apprentice. I knew that must have made her really happy. She asked about the academy, about what I was learning, and if I'd made any friends. I read the letter over three or four times before I folded it back up, tucking into the envelope, and slipped it under the corner of my mattress. I couldn't keep a smile off my face.

"So, everything's good with her?" Felix asked as he looked up from where he was studying again.

I sighed. "Yeah. Seems like it."

He nodded, smirking to himself like he thought it was funny. "Just look at that grin on your face. You should just tell her you like her, you know. Go ahead and get it out of the way before some other guy snaps her up."

I glared at him tiredly. "I told you, we're not like that. She doesn't—" I paused to think. "What do you mean snaps her up?"

Felix shrugged some. "You know, if she's pretty, you're probably not the only one who's going to notice her. It's all about timing, my friend."

That didn't sit too well with me, not that there was a single thing I could do about it. I sat up, pretending to study while I mulled it over. I didn't really know if I liked her or not. She'd been a friend, my only friend, up until recently. She was one of the few people I knew I could really trust. To tell her that I liked her would change everything, and not necessarily for the better.

When Felix went to sleep, I took out a clean piece of parchment and wrote a letter back to her. Since I'd come here, there had been plenty of time to practice writing. My spelling was still a little wonky sometimes, but it was much better than before.

I told her everything I could think of about the academy. I told her about Sile, and all the rigorous morning drills he made us do. I told her about Mavrik, and how together we'd saved Sile from being killed when his saddle malfunctioned. I told her about Felix, who was becoming more like an annoying older brother than a classmate. I told her about how he'd rescued me from being bullied a few times, and how he liked to tease me about everything. Finally, I told her that I liked it here. It was hard. Every day was tougher than the one before it, but I really did like it. I liked feeling like I had a purpose, and a future to look forward to. Even if only a few of these dragonriders liked me, I could deal with that. I could be happy anyway.

I paused to think about what else I should say. Felix thought I needed to tell her that I liked her, but I still wasn't sure about that. Leaving the letter unfinished, I folded the paper up and tucked it under the bed with the one she'd sent me. I would just have to think about it some more.

When it came to Katty, things had always been clear to me before. She was my very best friend, and definitely someone I cared about. But asking myself if I liked her the way Felix was talking about meant I'd be putting all that on the line if she didn't feel the same way. I just wasn't sure I was ready to risk that yet.

twelve

The day before the annual officer's ball, all our training was suspended for preparations. There were no morning drills, no pushups, and definitely no academics for us. The older students and officers had to have their formal armor refitted, polished, and perfected, so the hallways of the dorm were filled with the smell of shoe polish and clean laundry.

As fledglings, we didn't have anything like that yet. Instead, Sile came into our dorm room with a bag filled with new navy blue tunics that had the king's golden eagle stitched on the shoulders and breast, long black capes with a gold-colored chain around the neck, knee-high black boots, and black pants. There was a set for each of us, and Sile told us to go ahead and try everything on to make sure it fit.

"Can't have you two looking like bums at Duke Brinton's estate," Sile grumbled. He came over and started adjusting the collar of my tunic, then did the same to Felix's.

"Is that who's hosting it? Brinton? Well, at least there'll be a lot of wine." Felix snorted. "Duke Brinton loves his vineyards more than his own children. He talks about them like they were people instead of a bunch of plants. You should hear him at dinner. Just on and on—there's no stop to it. About the leaves, and the grapes, and how he's perfected the aging process. And his son, there's a real piece of work. You may have been born a halfbreed, Jae, but be glad you never had to endure a play date with Fredrick Brinton."

I snickered, and Sile cast us both a dangerous look. "Just keep your thoughts to yourself when you're at his estate, am I understood? No talking with the distinguished guests. No drinking. No dancing. You're there to help ladies from carriages into the ballroom, not flirt with them. You're there to serve wine, not drink any. This is a night for men, so remember your place, boys."

I was actually getting excited about it now. There would be food there unlike anything I'd ever tasted before. Even if most of the people there looked at me as if I were a cockroach, I was still going to enjoy it. I was still a fledgling dragonrider—so they couldn't exactly kick me out.

When we had packed our new uniforms up, with Sile standing over us, watching to make sure we didn't leave anything behind, we went to bed early. Everyone else did, too. For once, it was Felix who was too restless to sleep. He kept me up with his excited whispering, going on about Brinton's obnoxious fat son, Fredrick, and how his wife had a hooked nose and nasally laugh. I was relieved when he finally drifted off and I heard him start to snore. It didn't take me any time at all to fall asleep, too.

The call to arms sounded, and purely out of habit, I was already awake. Felix had no trouble sleeping in the extra few hours, though. He was still snoring and drooling, so I just finished my letter to Katty.

I promised her I'd come to visit as soon as I could, told her how I hoped to get another letter from her soon, and ended it at that. No emotional gushes or confessions of liking anyone. I just wasn't willing to risk it. In the whole world, I could count the number of people I could call friends on one hand, and one of them was a dragon. I didn't want to do anything to jeopardize the relationship I had with her. At least, not yet.

When Felix woke up, we started to get ready to go. We put on our fledgling's armor, grabbed our bags, and started down toward the Roost. It didn't take much time to get ready to leave, but it was really crowded. Every other rider in the academy was in the process of leaving, too. All around us, riders were fixing their saddles, tying down their bags, and taking off into the sky. Some of them had already left and were on their way to the east.

Sile was waiting for us. We hurried through fitting on our own saddles, tying down all our bags, and taking off. With the ocean to our backs, and the sun rising over the mountains before us, we started for Duke Brinton's estate.

A few twilight stars were still glittering in the west when Blybrig Academy emptied of all its dragonriders into the morning sky. It was an incredible thing to see. All around me in the sky were magnificent dragons and proud knights in gleaming armor. There were more than a hundred in total, all heading toward the break of day. And the best part was, I was one of them.

It was almost a full day of riding over mountains frosted with snow, steep desert canyons, lush green valleys, and rolling grasslands to get to Brinton's estate. We didn't even stop to rest, and by the time we could see the city below, my rear end was sore from sitting in the saddle for so long. We circled in a pattern, following Sile as he signaled to us that we were landing in waves, five at a time. I guessed that was to keep from overwhelming the

Duke's front door with a flock of dragons.

Duke Brinton was opening his enormous home and all its rooms to us. All the dragonriders from Blybrig were staying with him until tomorrow morning. It was an honor to spend the night in a noble's house. Even if they made me sleep in the stable with the horses, it would probably still be the nicest place I had ever stayed in.

We kept circling in a tight pattern until it was our turn to land and quickly unpack our bags before sending our dragons back into the air. They'd hang around in the area, waiting for us, but there was nowhere to stable them here. Besides, keeping dragons around livestock was generally a bad idea. Even tame dragons got hungry.

I stood back, watching Mavrik take to the air and soar skyward like a huge, blue-scaled eagle. He was so powerful and majestic, and seeing him join the flock of dragons in the air, swirling in a giant circular column like buzzards over a kill, was amazing. I still wasn't used to it, and it still took my breath away.

"Come on, we've gotta get ready!" Felix gave me a nudge and nodded toward the door.

Brinton's estate looked like a massive castle made of stacked white stone. There must have been a thousand rooms with gleaming windows on every side. The front lawn was like a front field, and in the center was a huge lake with white swans paddling around on it. In the back, there were acres upon acres of vineyards, stretching as far as I could see across the rolling landscape.

Two maids in matching blue and white dresses were holding the front doors open for all the dragonriders to come inside. As soon as we were inside, I forgot to look anywhere but up. The ceilings were incredibly tall, and painted with images of clouds, angels, and the old gods from the old fables doing battle with mythical beasts. I noticed that one of the demonic monsters looked a lot like a gray elf, only with pointy teeth and glowing yellow eyes.

The windows stretched up the walls, and chandeliers made of glittering crystal looked big enough to kill a few people if they happened to fall. Porcelain pots squatted on the floor, so big I could have climbed inside one to hide, but instead they were filled with blossoming fruit trees that made the air smell sweet. I felt totally out of place as I stood with my bag in one hand, and my helmet under my other arm.

Felix kept nudging me to keep me moving, and we followed Sile into the house, through the long hallways, up a grand staircase, to the east wing where we dragonriders were staying for the night. Maids dressed in that same blue and white dress went back and forth past us, and one paused to let us into a large suite that was for the three of us.

Sile waved us off as soon as he sat his bags down. "I've got to run a few errands before I dress. Go ahead and clean yourselves up. Try not to get into any trouble. In fact, just don't leave this room until I get back," he commanded before he went back outside.

The room was as big as Ulric's whole house, and then some. It had four bedrooms and a washroom attached to a big sitting room. One whole wall of the main room was entirely covered by a window that looked out onto a beautiful garden three storeys down. There was a big silver platter of fruit, cheese, a whole table of desserts set out for us to eat, and a fully stocked wine bar. Felix was eyeing that as I went from room to room, checking things out.

I couldn't believe I'd actually have a room all to myself. Not just a cot, or a shared room; I'd have my own bedroom with a double bed, soft sheets, and fluffy pillows. It was surreal, and I was afraid to touch anything for fear I'd get it dirty.

"He's gone to get his family, you know. The wives always come to this kind of thing. They love the show." Felix was leaning in the doorway, looking around at the glamorous bedroom. "So what do you think?"

I turned to look back at him. "About what?"

He waved a finger in a circle, gesturing the suite we'd be staying in for the next day.

"It's incredible." I couldn't hide my amazement. "Do you live in a house like this? Your father is a duke, too, isn't he?"

Felix shrugged like it wasn't a big deal. "Bigger, actually. But not nearly as gaudy. Brinton's family manages much smaller area, so I guess he feels like he has something to prove. My family line is much older. You know, there's a slim chance I could even be heir to the throne someday. King Felix. Sounds good, eh?"

I smirked and rolled my eyes at him, setting my bag down and beginning to take out the pieces of my uniform for the night. "No wonder you were excited about this. I'm actually kind of looking forward to it, now."

"Told you so." He smiled back at me, giving me a mischievous wink before he went to his own room to get ready. "And the real party hasn't even started yet."

I washed up, scrubbing dirt from my face and hands and neck, and combing my hair to make sure it covered my pointed ears before I got dressed. I checked in the big floor mirror in my room to make sure my collar was straight, and there wasn't a wrinkle out of place.

Sile came back in a hurry. He was alone, and didn't look very happy. He started rushing through his own preparations, cursing and muttering under his breath as he fought to get his cape buckled onto the pauldrons of his shoulder armor. As I finished getting ready, I wandered out into the parlor to watch him fighting to get his cape situated.

"Is everything all right, sir?" I dared to ask.

He didn't stop to look at me, finally getting the cape on right, and going on to hurriedly buckle up his beautifully engraved vambraces onto his forearms. "My wife has decided to stay at home. She's late on in her pregnancy, and just can't stomach to travel this far. But she sent our oldest child here with a nanny, and now the nanny's come down with some kind of stomach bug. She's emptying her guts, and it doesn't look like she'll be able to take care of herself for the rest of the night, let alone anyone else. So I'm left with an unchaperoned kid to worry with when I'm already supposed to be babysitting you two. I tried to find Brinton to ask him about using one of his own girls as a nanny, but of course he's nowhere to be found. Not that I blame him. There'll be about five hundred officers in attendance tonight, total. The whole house is in an uproar. He's got his hands full."

Sile had never mentioned his family to us before. I didn't even know he had a wife or any children. He was still growling and muttering under his breath while he finished getting dressed. "I can't just haul a kid around all night. I don't know why she'd even bother to send Beck at all," he grumbled. "She knows young kids aren't welcomed at events like this. It's not a play date."

"I could do it, sir." I offered before I even think it through.

Sile stopped in the middle of fastening his last buckle to frown at me. "Do what?"

"Watch after your son. Beck, right?" I clarified. "I've got two younger siblings, so I'm used to taking care of kids." That wasn't exactly true. Whenever I'd been forced to watch Emry and Lin, it always ended badly. They did everything they could to get me into trouble, and I was helpless to stop them because I was outnumbered. But one kid? Surely I could handle just one.

He narrowed his eyes, and opened his mouth like he was going to protest, but the door to our suite opened. One of the other instructors stuck his head into the room long enough to tell Sile we were ten minutes away from needing to report for presentation. We were out of time.

Growling more angry words under his breath, Sile shot me a quick glare. I could already tell, just by the look on his face, that I'd just blown my chance at seeing the officer's ball. I was going to be on babysitting duty for the night.

"Fine, you'll have to do. I'm out of time and out of options. You have to stay in the room, am I understood? No roaming the halls. I'll make sure there's a servant on call, in case you need anything," Sile told me as he ran out the door again.

All the air rushed out of me as soon as he shut the door. I deflated. I'd come all this way for nothing. I tried to tell myself it was for the best. I would probably cause more problems than I'd solve. Me working around nobles was the perfect recipe for disaster. I could just see some dainty noble girl screaming in horror when I tried to help her down out of her carriage.

Felix came out of his room already dressed and ready to go. He noticed my gloomy appearance right away. "What's wrong?"

"I'm not going," I told him bluntly. "I'm staying here in the room to babysit Sile's son."

"What?!" Felix's expression was pure horror. "That's what nannies are for! Don't tell me he didn't bring someone to look after his brat? Wait—did you say son?"

"He did bring a nanny, but she's sick. There's no one else to watch him. It's fine, Felix. Don't make a big show. I offered to stay behind and do it." I shook my head, wishing I'd just let Sile handle the problem himself.

He stared at me like I was dumber than he'd originally thought, and rolled his eyes. "You need to learn when to pocket that conscience of yours, you know. Or at least keep your mouth shut."

"Yeah, well there's nothing I can do about it now. It's fine—I'll be fine." I tried to sound confident. I knew I could babysit. That wasn't a problem. This kid couldn't possibly be worse than Emry and Lin were. "Besides, at least it's a boy, right? I'll just teach him to sword fight or something."

The suite door opened. Sile came back into the room holding the hand of a girl who looked only a little younger than I was. She was wearing a simple sky blue dress, and her dark hair was tied into a braid down her back. She had her father's dark green eyes, and there were a lot of freckles across her nose and cheeks. My heart sank to the bottom of my stomach. Suddenly I was having horrible flashbacks to all the times Emry and Lin had gotten me into huge trouble.

"B-Beck?" I looked at Sile for an explanation. Beck sounded like a boy's name, but Beck was obviously anything but a boy.

He just smirked like he'd fooled me good. It was as though he were daring me to withdraw my offer to babysit her. "Beckah. We call her Beck for short. Is there a problem?"

My mouth was hanging open. I was totally stunned as I stood there, looking between him and the girl. She still didn't say a word. I was shocked, but I wasn't stupid enough to take back my offer just because it was a girl instead of a boy. I figured trying something like that would probably make me look like a hypocrite … and Sile would just make me do it anyway.

"N-no sir, no problem," I finally managed to answer.

Felix snickered. I saw him grinning at me out of the corner of my eye. Somehow, I got the feeling he'd known Beck was a girl all along and just didn't want to ruin the surprise. He wasn't even doing a good job of stifling his laughter as he ducked out of the room, giving me an exaggerated little wave on his way. I guess he thought this was hilarious. He'd never let me live it down.

thirteen

I was officially on my own.

Felix and Sile both left right after another maid came in with two trunks full of Beckah's stuff. Sile only gave me a few instructions before he rushed out the door: no leaving the room, no breaking anything, and Beckah had to be in bed in three hours. Now I was standing before a girl who still didn't look convinced that I could be trusted, even though Sile had assured her I was harmless. She looked at me warily, like she might run if I made one wrong move.

I wasn't sure what to say. She was definitely older than my sisters, but still younger than I was. I had no idea what girls her age liked to do. Well, other than torture me occasionally.

"Um, so your name is Beckah?" I asked her. Since I was small for my age, I was just about looking at her eye-to-eye.

She just blinked and didn't say anything. I could see traces of Sile in her expressions, especially when she frowned at me. He definitely had to claim her as his child.

"I'm Jae," I told her.

She was beginning to hedge a few steps closer. I noticed how her eyes were quick, and darted over me curiously. You could just tell by the way she was examining me that she was smart, probably a lot smarter than I was.

"Daddy won't let me go to the party with him," she said at last. "He says it's for adults only, but you were going to get to go."

"Well, not really," I explained. "I was going to have to work. You know, serve food and open doors. Not exactly much fun. Maybe it'll be more fun to just stay here, after all. They left plenty of food in here."

I saw her smile for a moment, just a little bit. It was like watching a star shine out from behind a veil of clouds. I knew Sile would beat me within an inch of my life for thinking it, but I couldn't help but notice that she was really pretty. There was something earthy about the mixture of her green eyes, dark hair, and the freckles sprinkled over her nose. Something about her, for whatever reason, reminded me of my mother. Maybe it was that curious twinkle in her eyes.

"You're half elf, aren't you?" she asked me suddenly.

I felt my heart twist in my chest so hard it hurt. This was the moment I'd been dreading, because pretty much everyone felt the same way about halfbreeds like me. I just nodded and braced myself, fully expecting her to give me a look of disgust.

Suddenly her smile came back, spreading over her face and making her cheeks get rosy. "That's what daddy told me. He said your momma was a gray elf." She sounded curious. She started coming closer to me, and I was immediately on red alert. I stiffened, staring at her uncomfortably as she looked me over from head to toe. "What was she like? I've never met a gray elf before."

"Not like what you've heard, I'm sure." I was quick to defend my mother's honor. "She was the kindest person I've ever known. And she could grow anything."

Beckah was nibbling on her bottom lip as she reached out to touch my hair. I couldn't help myself; I flinched away. Her expression was as surprised by my reaction as I was that she'd actually wanted to touch me. And then, for whatever reason, she looked sad.

"Okay, then. We'll just have our own party here," she announced. "Since daddy won't let us join his. What's for dessert?"

I wasn't so sure about this anymore. Beckah was the strangest girl I'd ever met, which was saying something since I'd grown up with two goblins for sisters. But Beckah wasn't like them. She wasn't mean to me, and she didn't seem to be disgusted by me, either. Just like her father, she seemed to think I was interesting.

There was a big tray of desserts already set up and waiting for us, and she breezed right past the rest of the food and headed straight for it. I watched her eat three big bowls of fruit drizzled in chocolate, honey, candied nuts, and whipped cream. I just nibbled on a peach. I had a good idea what rich food like that would do to my stomach, and that wasn't how I wanted to spend the evening.

She kept me distracted, anyway. She asked dozens of questions about my mother, my father, and the academy. It was a little strange. I assumed Sile would have told her most of this stuff already, but she seemed really interested to learn anything she could about dragons and the academy.

"Daddy doesn't come home much, anymore. He's busy with training all the time," she said with a mouthful of food. "It makes momma really angry. That's why she said I had to come, even if daddy doesn't want me here. She said he doesn't spend enough time with me. I wish I could go with him, just once. I'd like to see the dragons."

"Maybe he'll bring you when you're older." I couldn't keep from smiling at her. She just said whatever crossed her mind. I'd never met anyone like that before. "What about you? Do you wish he was home more?"

She shrugged and looked down into her third bowl of dessert. "I guess. But even when he is home, it's like his mind is far away. He doesn't really see us. We just make him frustrated and upset when he's home. It's always been like that. He and momma fight a lot. I don't think she's very happy about the new baby. I've heard her crying at night. I think she wishes daddy would just quit being a dragonrider and come back home."

I could see the pain on her face, even if she didn't realize she was showing it. I knew how she felt. Wanting her dad's approval, or just a little of his time, was something I understood completely. "It's not your fault, Beckah. It's nobody's fault. He's got a lot to think about. His job is stressful, and dangerous. I'm sure he loves you."

"Are you going to be like that, when you're grown up?" she pointed an accusing gaze at me suddenly.

I wasn't sure how to answer that. I just sat there staring at her, and tried to think of a good reply, with my mouth hanging open. I couldn't get any sound to come out.

"Don't be that way, okay? You're really nice, I can tell. So don't be like that. Don't forget about everyone else—

especially the ones who need you the most." She stood up to refill her bowl, and it seemed like she just wanted to get away from me for a minute. She was upset. I wasn't very perceptive, and I knew nothing about girls, but even I could tell she wasn't happy. Talking about her family made her upset. She wanted to go to the ball, but not for the same reason everyone else did. She just wanted to be near Sile.

"So what else do the adults do at parties? Other than eat too much dessert?" I gave her a hopeful smile, and tried to change the subject.

Beckah sighed loudly. "There's always dancing, and they stand around and gossip about each other." She came back to sit on the floor next to me, a little too close for my comfort. "Sometimes the men fight, but only when they've had too much wine and decide to act stupid."

I smirked; that reminded me of Felix for some reason. "I don't know any gossip, or how to dance."

Her eyes popped open wide, and she grinned at me like she had a brilliant idea. Grabbing my wrist, she bounded to her feet and started pulling me toward the door eagerly. "Come on! I know where we can go and see the real party! I'll teach you how to dance."

Suddenly Sile's warning that we should stay in this room was ringing in my ears. I dug my heels in. "We can't go out. Your dad said—"

"My daddy just doesn't want me to bother him. That's how it always is. But we won't get caught. He won't ever know we're there. I promise! Please?" She begged, and puckered her bottom lip out some. "Don't you want to at least see the party?"

Of course I did. I also didn't want to imagine what Sile would do to me if I broke any rules—especially ones about his daughter. I started to shake my head.

Then Beckah gave me the best begging face I'd ever seen. Her big, round green eyes blinked up at me sadly, and I folded like a wet napkin. I was helpless against that kind of manipulation, especially when her chin started to tremble.

"Fine, fine. Just a quick look, but then we come straight back." I surrendered.

She started pulling me toward the door, opening it to lean out and peer left and right before we went outside. I got a sick feeling in the pit of my stomach that this wasn't going to end well. Even though the hallways were empty, I could still hear the sounds of laughter and music echoing faintly like whispers over the marble floors.

Beckah led the way through rooms decorated with expensive rugs and furniture. The further we went, the louder the music became, although it seemed to be coming from everywhere. We went through doors, down stairs, up stairs, and I was beginning to worry we'd never find our way back again. Reaching to grasp her hand tightly, I reeled myself in closer to her. I couldn't get my bearings in this place at all, and if I lost her, I'd never find my way back to our room alone.

"How do you know where we're going?" I whispered. We'd come up several narrow flights of stairs, and I was out of breath.

Beckah stopped on a landing where a single door was hidden in the shadows. She started opening it, and peeking through the crack. Light spilled in from the other side, and suddenly the sound of the music was much louder. It seemed to be coming from below us.

"Haven't you ever been in an estate like this before? All rich people's houses are basically the same, you know. Big, fancy, and with lots of hidden passages for servants," she whispered back. She opened the door just enough for us to slip through, and quickly shut it again.

A broad open space stretched out before us. Overhead, the wooden rafters were visible going up into the gloom. Brilliant golden light bled up through the cracks in the floorboards, shining from the ballroom below. There were ghostly pieces of furniture standing along the walls, covered up with white sheets. I started to realize this was a storage room.

I could hear the music, the sounds of laughter and conversation, and even smell the food coming from party under our feet. It filled me with excitement, even if I was still worried about being caught up here. Neither one of us could resist the urge to squat down and peer through one of the cracks.

The ballroom was massive, sparkling with the light from big crystal chandeliers, and filled with beautiful people that stood around talking, drinking wine, or were twirling on the dance floor. There were officers with all kinds of uniforms. Ladies wore fancy ball gowns encrusted with jewels, and white gloves up to their elbows. I saw the other fledgling dragonriders carrying silver platters with wine glasses on them.

"Look, there's daddy!" Beckah whispered, pointing toward a corner where there was a large group of high-ranking dragonriders gathered. They were laughing and drinking, probably telling war stories.

For some reason, seeing everyone like that made me sad. I sat back on my knees and sighed. I couldn't help but wonder if this was as close as I'd ever get to a party like that. Granted, this was a lot closer than I'd ever been before. But was I really just kidding myself? Did I really have a place with people like that?

"Jae?" Beckah was looking at me with an unhappy quirk to her mouth. "I'm sorry you got stuck with me, instead of going to the party."

It wasn't hard to smile at her. "No, it's not that. I just

always end up wondering how I'll ever fit in with people like that. It was … kind of a fluke that I even ended up being a dragonrider at all."

"Well, do you like it?" she asked me frankly.

"Like what?"

"Being a dragonrider?" she asked again.

I nodded. Just thinking about it made my heart beat faster. "Yeah. I love it."

She shrugged a little. "Then nothing else matters. Who cares about fitting in with them? If it's something you really care about, then it shouldn't matter what anyone else thinks."

She sat back on her heels right across from me, looking me up and down with her intelligent green eyes. She was pretty sharp, for a kid. I had to give her credit for that. She really was a lot smarter than me, which was kind of scary.

"I guess you're right." I looked back down at the floor and the dancing couples far below. Maybe I'd never be one of them, but Beckah was right. Compared to the other places I could have ended up, this was a pretty great one to be in.

fourteen

"Let's dance," Beckah demanded as she stood, dusting off the front of her blue dress.

I stared up at her, and started trying to think of a good excuse not to. "I already told you I don't know how."

"And I said I would teach you, so come on!" She was relentless, and grabbed my arm to pull me back up. She took my hands and showed me how to stand so I was holding her. I did my best not to touch her any more than was absolutely necessary, but my face started to get hot right away. I wanted to pull away. I could just imagine Sile walking in just in time to see me dancing with his daughter.

"Daddy showed me how. Look, like this." She

coached me through a few wobbly dance steps with a big grin on her face.

After a few minutes of stepping on her feet, shuffling around, and feeling like an idiot, I was beginning to realize that I was a terrible dancer. But she didn't seem to mind, and so neither did I. She laughed, twirled, and refused to let me give up, even when I stepped on her toes. As long as she was having fun, that was all that mattered to me.

"You have to practice, Jae," she told me. I could tell she was teasing me a little. "You can't step on anyone's shoes next year. What if you squash some princess's toes?"

I smirked, and just rolled my eyes at her. "Right, because all the noble ladies will be lining up to dance with a halfbreed."

She flashed me a punishing look, and got a thoughtful twinkle in her eyes. "I'll dance with you. I'll be fifteen next year, so I can come to the party, too. Daddy won't be able to just dump me on some nanny—no offense."

"None taken. But for what it's worth, this is a lot more fun than serving drinks." I twirled her again. I could tell that was her favorite, and I liked it because it meant I didn't have to move around much.

Beckah's cheeks got a little red, and she stuck her tongue out at me. When she stopped twirling, she let go of my hand and stood there for a moment. It got really awkward. She was just looking at me with this weird expression, nibbling on her bottom lip. It made me nervous.

"We should go back, huh?" she mumbled.

I was starting to think that was good idea. "Yeah, probably."

She led the way back out of the storage room, down the stairs, and into the hallways of Duke Brinton's estate. I still couldn't figure out where we were, or which way we were supposed to be going, but I trusted her. She held my hand tightly, her small fingers laced through mine. It made me feel strange, no matter how hard I tried to ignore it. I wasn't sure if I liked it, or if it just made me really nervous.

We were as fast as shadows as we crept through the house. We slipped from room to room, taking the shortcuts through empty servant tunnels. We hid from passing maids and butlers by ducking into dark corners whenever we heard footsteps or voices coming too close.

It felt like we were getting close when we came to a dimly lit hallway that was very close to the ballroom where the party was still going strong. I could hear the music clearly, even feel it vibrating the floor under my feet. I could smell the food, the perfume of the flowers, and see the bright golden light gleaming far away down the hall. Voices echoed toward us, but it wasn't the sounds of laughter and excited conversation I'd expected to hear.

Beckah stopped so suddenly I crashed into her back. Her eyes got wide.

Then I heard it, too. It was Sile's voice. He was shouting at the top of his lungs, and it sounded like he was arguing with someone.

Beckah just stood there frozen with her eyes as big as saucers. I reacted in an instant, and grabbed her by the back of her dress to pull her into the shadows to hide. We stood stock still as the voices came closer. I held my breath, keeping a firm grip on Beckah with an arm around her waist to keep her from slipping into view.

Five people passed us. Four men all dressed in black, their faces covered with masks painted white with two red lines over the eyes. Sile was in the middle of them, and they were shoving him along with his hands tied behind his back. One of them was holding the point of a long black dagger against his side.

"You cowards," Sile was growling at them. "You really think killing me is going to make any difference? What that madman has done won't be absolved with my death! It will tear this kingdom apart!"

The masked men didn't answer. They just kept shoving him onward, jabbing at him threateningly with that dagger.

"You can take me all the way to Halfax and it will

make no difference!" He continued to fight against them, struggling to get free. "Don't you get it?! This is what happens to those who tamper with gods!"

Beckah flinched against me. I could feel her shaking with panic. I slapped a hand over her mouth to hold her back before she could move or make any noise. If they found us, then they might kill us, too. She let out a faint, muffled whimper against my palm.

The five men disappeared into the dark, never stopping once. They didn't see us. Once I was sure they were out of earshot, I let Beckah go. She jerked away from me violently, and started to sprint after them. I ran after her.

"What are you doing?!" I whispered as I snatched her by the wrist, forcing her to stop.

"They're going to kill my daddy! Didn't you hear? We have to do something!" She looked back at me with a furious, pleading expression. There were tears running down her cheeks. "Help me, Jae. Please!"

"We can't just go after them, not by ourselves! Look at us, Beckah, we can't fight men like that! We have to find some of the other officers. Come on!" I started to pull her in the opposite direction, back toward the party. She didn't fight me, but I could hear her sobbing. If we could find another officer—someone trained to handle this kind of thing—then maybe we could stop those men before they did something terrible to Sile.

"W-who were they, Jae? Who were those men?" Beckah cried as I pulled her along after me, sprinting for the ballroom.

I didn't know. I'd never seen anyone wear masks like that before. My head was swirling with confusion and terror as we ran toward burning light that poured into the hallway. It felt like we were running toward the gates of heaven in some kind of nightmare. No matter how hard I pumped my legs, it still felt like I was moving in slow motion.

When we finally got to the doorway of the ballroom, the roar of the crowd and the surge of the music stopped me dead. I was dazed, panicked, and searching for someone I knew. But I didn't see a single familiar face in the crowd. There were hundreds of people all around, and none of them even looked my way.

"Jae, we have to hurry!" Beckah pleaded.

I clenched my teeth and nodded. There wasn't time to stand here and wait for someone to notice us. I went up to the first officer I could find, and started tugging on his sleeve. "Sir, excuse me! I have an emergency!"

The officer glared down at me, brushing me away angrily. "My wine cup is fine, boy. Move along." He didn't look back down at me again.

I tried other officers, and one after another, but they all ignored me in pretty much the same way. Not one would even give me a second look. They couldn't be bothered to step away from their conversations with the ladies, or their cups filled with Brinton's precious wine. Beckah was sobbing hysterically, and I was beginning to get frustrated.

In a moment of desperation and pure stupidity, I spotted Academy Commander Rayken standing with his wife and a few other noblemen, and marched right up to him. I pulled on his sleeve like I had the others, but this time I shouted at the top of my lungs. "Commander Rayken! Someone has kidnapped Lieutenant Derrick!"

The people around us went silent for a moment, turning stare down at me. It must have scared Beckah, because she pressed herself up against my back, and squeezed my hand even harder. I could feel her trembling.

Academy Commander Rayken looked at me like he'd just found a stain on his shirt. He scowled, and didn't say a word. He didn't have to; I could tell he was waiting for me to explain myself.

"I saw it myself, sir. Four men in white masks took him just a moment ago. He was yelling, but no one else could hear." I started to get nervous. Maybe going up to Commander Rayken like that had been a huge mistake. He could still kick me out of the academy if he wanted to, and he was probably the last person in the world who would believe a word I said.

He just scowled at me even harder, like I was wasting his time, and rolled his eyes. "What you're describing is the king's private guard, and as you can see, there are none of them present because they *only* accompany the king himself when he travels. You're mistaken. Lieutenant Derrick is here, somewhere in the ballroom. I saw him not an hour ago." He growled down at me, making me back up a few feet. "Go back to your duties, fledgling, before I lose my patience."

My heart sank to the soles of my boots. I wasn't going to get any help from these people. They didn't believe me, just like before when Sile's saddle had been tampered with. Once again, it was up to me to do something to save Lieutenant Derrick.

So I made another desperate, stupid decision that was probably going to end up costing me more than I wanted to lose.

fifteen

"**B**eckah, you have to take me up to the roof. You know how to get there, don't you?" I turned to face her as soon as we got out of the ballroom.

She hesitated, looking at me with wide eyes filled with tears. I could see the fear on her face. Her chin was trembling when she finally nodded. "I-I think so. But why?"

I wasn't sure exactly what was going on with Sile, but it just had to be something bad for these guys to come after him twice. After what happened with the saddle, I couldn't afford to take this lightly. Lives were at stake. And just like last time, no one else believed me. So if *I* didn't do something, Sile might die.

I was just one fledgling with no real training, so it was going to take something pretty radical to make any difference at all. Fortunately, radical was my middle name. Or at least, it was about to be.

"I'm going to save your dad, Beckah. Don't worry." I tried to reassure her. "So let's go, and hurry!"

Beckah led the way through the duke's mansion at a sprint, and I actually had a hard time keeping up with her this time. She was faster than she looked, and I was out of breath as we went up staircase after staircase, climbing the levels of the estate toward the roof. We dashed past maids and servants, who stopped to stare or yelled at us to slow down.

A few things started to look familiar as we came close to the suite we were supposed to be staying in for the night. I recognized a big oil painting and a small orange tree growing out of a big porcelain pot right outside the door of our room as we ran past. It gave me a sick feeling to think of what was going to happen when the other officers, especially Commander Rayken, figured out Sile and I were missing. I could probably kiss the academy goodbye. So much for my bright new future.

"Jae?" Someone shouted my name and I screeched to a halt to see who it was. My heart was hammering in my chest, and I half hoped it would be Sile. Even if he was furious with me for leaving the room with his daughter,

I'd just be so relieved that he was okay.

But it wasn't Sile.

Felix was leaning out of a doorway back down the hall, and his face was smeared with something red. I couldn't tell what it was until he started walking toward me. It looked like lipstick. His hair was all messed up, too.

"What're you doing?" He frowned at me suspiciously. "I thought Sile said you weren't supposed to be out here? He's gonna chew your head off if he catches you." He was one to be talking. Out of the corner of my eye, I saw a noble girl in a party dress run out of the room he'd been in.

"Jae!" Beckah whimpered impatiently. We really didn't have time for this.

"I can't explain it to you now. Sile is in trouble again, and I have to go," I told him.

"Wait, what?" Felix looked stunned. "Go where? What's going on, Jae?"

"I can't, Felix. I'm sorry. There's no time." I shook my head, and turned to start running again.

I got about three feet away before I suddenly came to a jerking, choking stop. Felix had me by the back of my cape so that the chain drew up tight around my neck. He started dragging me back toward him, and when I saw his face again, he looked furious.

"Let me go!" I shouted at the top of my lungs. "Sile is going to die if you don't let me go!"

That definitely got his attention. Felix let me go right away, and just stood there, staring at me like I was out of my mind. "What are you talking about?"

I stumbled when he released my cape, and started taking steps back away from him. "I saw it, Felix. Four men in white masks kidnapped him from the ball. She saw it, too. This isn't a joke." I glared at him, and tried to look as confident as I could despite the fact that I was terrified about what I was about to do. "I tried telling Commander Rayken and the others, but they don't believe me—just like *you* didn't believe me last time. So it's up to me again. I'm going to save him, even if I have to do it alone."

I regretted bringing up the saddle incident, especially since Felix was my friend. I knew it'd probably make him angry, but I wanted him to take me seriously. I didn't stick around after that, just in case he tried to stop me. I ran back toward Beckah, who stood there waiting for me before she started sprinting down the hall again.

We took off into the duke's estate, and it wasn't until we were climbing another steep, spiraling staircase that I realized we weren't alone. Felix was right behind me. He wouldn't look right at me, even when I almost tripped over my own feet in surprise.

"What are you doing?" I gasped, trying to talk as I panted for breath.

Then Felix shot me a punishing glare, like I should have known better than to think he wouldn't believe me this time. "You really think I'm going to let you do something this stupid by yourself?"

I was about to say yes. Actually I'd expected him to laugh at me as I ran off to ruin my career and probably get myself killed in the process. But I couldn't catch my breath long enough to say anything else. Good thing Sile had been making us run all those laps, or I would have passed out.

Beckah led the way through the mansion, up to the top of one of the towering spires that had a cone-shaped roof. It was a watchtower with a huge lantern in the top to light the grounds below, like some kind of a really tall, skinny lighthouse. But there weren't any guards watching it tonight because of the party. In fact, when we finally made it to the landing at the top of the stairs, the door was locked with a big iron padlock. Beckah pulled on it, clawed at it, and finally let out a little scream of panic when it wouldn't budge.

"Oh would you just move?" Felix grumbled, shoving her out of the way so hard she bounced off my chest and almost fell down the stairs. Lucky for her, I was quick to catch her by the shoulders.

Felix pulled what looked like a small metal hairpin out of his pocket, and started poking it into the keyhole. It only took him a few minutes to pick the lock. When it sprang free, he pushed the wooden door open for us to go up into the chamber above.

The room at the top of the tower was round with open stone windows all the way around. We had an excellent view of how high up we were—which was really, really high. So high that it made my head swim at first, even though I had gotten pretty used to flying with Mavrik. The night air blew through the open arched windows, and since the lantern in the center wasn't lit, you could see thousands of stars glittering overhead.

"What now?" Felix came to stand beside me with his arms folded.

I started walking toward one of the windows. "Just a crazy idea," I told him as I leaned out, looking at the ten-storey drop below.

It was pretty crazy to think that Mavrik would ever hear me, even way up here. I didn't even know where he was. And yet it had always seemed like he could understand it when I spoke to him, so it was worth a try. I had a strange feeling in my chest, like a hard knot of heat that tingled and made me shiver. I guessed it was just fear, or just a wild sense of desperation.

I took a deep breath, and climbed out onto the ledge.

The wind whipped in my hair, and tugged at my cape. Every time my boots slipped a little, my heart jumped into my throat.

"Jaevid?!" Felix was yelling at me. "Are you nuts? Get down from there!"

Beckah was yelling at me too, but I tuned them both out. I closed my eyes, and let my mind go quiet for a moment. I felt a strange sensation in my chest, like pressure, and a tingling of heat in the back of my mind. Then it was my turn to yell, and I screamed as loudly as I could. "*Mavrik! I need you!*"

At first, nothing happened. I started to feel like a real idiot, standing out there on that ledge, yelling for a dragon that couldn't hear me. Minutes went by, and I started to give up.

Then I heard him roar.

I opened my eyes, and saw two black shapes flapping toward us like shadows on the wind. Mavrik and Nova wheeled in circles around the tower, their wing beats like thunder in the air, as they tried to figure out how to get to us. The tower's cone-shaped roof was too small for them to land. It was time to earn that radical middle name.

I reached toward Beckah, offering her my hand. "Come on. You have to trust me!"

She looked absolutely terrified. Her eyes were as big as saucers, and she trembled as she took a few small steps toward me. Even Felix looked like he thought I'd totally lost it as he stood there with his mouth hanging open.

I caught Beckah by the hand and started to bring her in closer, helping her climb out onto the ledge with me. That's when Felix finally woke up from his trance of shock and awe. Suddenly, he grabbed Beckah by the back of the dress before she could climb out the window.

"She's not coming with us," he declared. "It's too dangerous."

"What if those masked men come back for her? We can't just leave her—!" I started to argue, but Beckah cut me off.

"You're not leaving me behind!" She struggled against his hold on her dress, finally managing to squirm out of his grip. "He's my daddy. I'm going!"

Beckah didn't seem afraid anymore. She swung her legs over the side of the windowsill, and was hanging onto the ledge while the wind snatched at her skirts. She gave me a look of determination, like she was trying to convince me that she really wasn't scared.

I looped an arm around her waist, and pulled her toward me. I figured I had about two seconds before she got scared again and did something to mess up my aim. So before she could figure out what I was about to do, and right when Mavrik was circling back toward us … I jumped. I jumped off the ledge ten storeys in the air, and

I took her with me.

Beckah screamed, but I could barely hear her as the wind rushed past my ears. I just held onto her as tightly as I could as we fell, and braced myself for what was coming; either death from the fall or what I hoped would be a dragon catching us.

Mavrik did catch us. He came darting through the air, wings spread wide, and hovered just long enough for us to crash into him. We hit hard, and it knocked the breath out of me at first. I was dazed, relieved, and trying to get my bearings.

We landed on Mavrik's back just a few feet away from the saddle, and I started dragging Beckah toward it with all my might. She didn't fight me at all. In fact, she was clinging to my chest like some kind of frightened baby animal. I had to pry her off me when I finally got into the seat and crammed my feet down into the leg sheaths on either side of the saddle. With Beckah sitting in my lap, I kept one arm wrapped tightly around her waist, and finally got a chance to look back at Felix.

He was standing on the ledge now, looking at Nova as she circled around the tower. I saw him make some kind of prayer sign with his hand before he jumped. I heard him yell, saw him drop, and Nova dove after him with a trumpeting roar.

She was bigger and slower, so she missed him at first.

As she zoomed past, she stretched out one of her strong hind legs to snatch him out of the air by the boot. He hung upside down, screaming and flailing until Nova tossed him back up into the air like a cat playing with a dead mouse.

He flipped end over end, and came back down to land right in the saddle with a hard thud. He had his arms and legs wrapped around her scaly body, and sat there clinging to her until he finally realized he wasn't about to plummet to his death. Then he got himself situated in the saddle, and we veered away toward the horizon.

Where are we going? Felix asked me with the sign language we'd learned to use in the air.

I only had one free hand since I was hanging onto Beckah, but I still managed to sign back to him, *Halfax.*

I've got the lead, he signed. *We'll fly low and watch the roads. Maybe we can catch them before they get too far away.*

I nodded, and was glad to let him lead since I really had no idea how to get to Halfax from here. I was starting to let myself hope. If we could find Sile, then surely we could find some way to save him. Maybe, just maybe, this would work.

sixteen

It was a pretty good plan in theory. We were going to do low passes along the roads, looking for any sign of recent travelers and the men wearing white masks. But as the hours began to drag on, we had to broaden our search, and still didn't find any sign of them at all. It was as though they'd disappeared completely.

The sun was starting to rise, and the early morning wind was bitter cold. Beckah was shivering, and I could hear her teeth chattering. She definitely wasn't dressed for this altitude, so I took off my cape and wrapped it around her to keep her warm.

"Jae?" She whimpered and grabbed one of my hands as I reached around her for the saddle handles. "What if we can't find him?"

I clenched my teeth because now I was beginning to worry about the same thing. "We'll find him, Beckah." For her sake, I tried to sound sure about that. "Don't give up."

Felix and Nova swooped in close, and he started giving me hand signals again. *We need to land and come up with a new plan.*

Right, I agreed. *Let's stick close to the roads, just in case.*

He nodded, and Nova veered away to find a good place to land. Mavrik and I followed, keeping close on his tail. We found a good spot where the main road leading toward Halfax dipped down through some low marshlands. There were lots of big trees covered in hanging moss, and just enough room for the dragons to drop down and land. Our dragons could hunker down under the trees so no one could see them, even from the air. It was the perfect hiding spot to rest and keep a lookout for any passing traffic without giving ourselves away too easily.

As soon as we dismounted, the dragons rooted around in the mud to find places to lie down, but neither one of them looked happy about it. The mud stank like rotting compost, and it was slimy and thick. It was miserable to walk around in it because it would just about suck your boots right off your feet. Finally, we found a spot dry enough to at least sit down.

"If you're right about them going to Halfax, then they'll have to come by this way," Felix grumbled as he plopped down and started trying to rake the disgusting silt off his boots with a stick. "This is the only road through the marshlands. Any other way would take you days to get around it."

"I don't understand how we could have missed them. Maybe we should have been flying lower." I was helping Beckah hobble through the sludge. She had to hold her skirts up to keep from tripping, but they still got caked in mud.

"We should have been plenty low enough to see them on the road." Felix sighed as he gave up trying to get the mud off his shoes. He was leaning back against a tree trunk, staring up at the morning sky. "We have no armor, no weapons, and no food. This is definitely a new level of stupid for me."

I sat down beside Felix, and Beckah settled in right next to me. She leaned against me, and was already sound asleep before I had even gotten comfortable. It was weird to have her clinging to me like that.

"I didn't mean for you to come with me, Felix. I know this'll probably ruin my career and get me kicked out of the academy. I didn't want it to ruin everything for you, too," I told him. "If we get caught just blame it all on me, okay?"

He chuckled, and gave me a teasing punch to the arm. "Nice try, small fry. We're in this together. I couldn't let you run off and get yourself killed, not after what happened with the saddle last time. You're right. I should have believed you then. And I do believe you now."

I smirked back at him; that made me feel a little better. "So what's the plan?"

Felix let out another loud sigh, and put his head back against the tree trunk. "I was about to ask you the same thing. I guess you should tell me exactly what you saw, first."

So I did. I told him everything I could remember about sneaking out of the room, about seeing Sile with his hands bound, and the four men in white masks that had him at knifepoint. It hadn't looked good, and we'd lost critical time trying to find someone to help us.

"I know it sounds crazy," I said, trying to get comfortable with Beckah leaning against me. She was sleeping so hard she didn't even quit snoring when I pulled her legs over my lap so she was resting with her head against my shoulder.

"After what happened with the saddle, not really." Felix was chewing on the inside of his cheek, looking thoughtful. "The white masks do sound like the king's private guard, though. I've only ever seen them around when someone from the royal family is visiting. But, if anyone could pull off a kidnapping like that in the middle of a ball, it'd be them. They're an elite guard trained in extreme stealth and hand-to-hand combat. They're usually handpicked from the military, and then completely removed from society. No one knows much about them because everything about their training is totally secret. It's like a cult, I guess."

My heart sank a little. "Why would they want to kidnap Sile?"

Felix just shook his head, and we both sat there for a long time in silence. This was bad. If these guys were the king's elite guards, what chance did a couple of fledgling dragonriders stand against them? Even if we could find them, we probably wouldn't be able to free Sile. We really had no idea what we were getting ourselves into.

"How did you do that earlier?" Felix asked suddenly. He was staring over at me with a weird look on his face. "How did you call Mavrik to you? And from that distance? It was incredible! I've never even heard of someone doing that before."

I blushed. "I don't know. It just ... felt like what I had to do. It was just an idea. I wasn't even sure he'd hear me."

"You're really weird sometimes, you know that?" Felix laughed, but I could still see that strange look in his eyes. It almost seemed like he was a little bit afraid of me now. I wasn't sure how to feel about it either, but it kind of bothered me that he seemed disturbed by it.

Felix offered to take the first watch while I slept. As much as I wanted to rest, I just couldn't get comfortable. Every little noise woke me up, and I had terrible dreams of darkness, and creatures slithering through the marshes toward us. When it was my turn to keep watch, I knew I had to get up just to walk off my nerves. I carefully moved Beckah over so she could lean against Felix instead.

"Sile's gonna kill us for bringing her along," Felix muttered sleepily as he licked his thumb and wiped some mud off her cheek. "He won't want her around the dragons. He probably doesn't want her around us, either, but I guess he didn't have much of a choice when you volunteered to watch her tonight."

I was surprised he knew anything about her, especially since Sile had never mentioned her before to me. "How do you know that?"

"That's how it always is, Jae. You can't be a dragonrider and be a family man, too. Trust me. If dragonriders do get married, it never lasts long." Felix had a hollow sound to his voice, like he sort of understood. "If you bring people you care about into a world of war and danger, then someone is going to get hurt. Usually, it's us. We have one of the most dangerous jobs anyone can have. Most dragonriders just decide it's better not to have people in your life like that—people you can't stand to lose or who depend on you. That's why you'll see a lot of them with broken families, more than one failed marriage, or no family at all."

As I stood there over them, watching Beckah sleep against Felix's shoulder, I started thinking about what she'd told me about her own family. "She said her parents aren't getting along. That's why she ended up at the duke's house in the first place."

Felix looked down at her, too, frowning like he felt bad for her. "I guess those of us from noble families kind of dodge the worst of it … because we don't expect our parents to pay much attention to us anyway. I mean, my dad was never around to begin with, even though he's not a dragonrider. He has always had problems with his vision, so he never would have made it through the academy. It didn't make any difference, though. He's never had any time for me." He hesitated, and I could tell just by the way his expression darkened that he must have felt a lot of anger toward his father. "The worst part is being alone. She'll hate that, you know?"

I did know. I knew exactly what it meant to be alone. Finally, I thought I understood why Felix had wanted to be friends with me in the first place. I was probably the only one who could understand the value of having someone be there for you, especially when your family wasn't.

"Yeah, but we'll be there for her." I gave him a half-hearted smile. "Someone should be. It might as well be us."

Felix just smirked and closed his eyes. "Speak for yourself, nanny."

He had no room to be cracking jokes at me for babysitting. "Well, you still have lipstick on your face, you know." I snorted.

Felix started blushing and wiping his face. "Yeah yeah, you just go keep watch and let me sleep. We'll start the search again in an hour. Those guards couldn't have just vanished. Maybe we just missed them. We'll check every road between here and Halfax if we have to. "

I tried to let that give me some hope as I walked away. We weren't giving up yet. There was still time to find Sile. It was already late in the morning, and my stomach was growling. The few hours of restless sleep I'd gotten only made me even more tired, but I knew there was no way I would be able to relax until I knew Sile was alive.

I paced a wide circle around where they were sleeping, keeping them in eyeshot at all times while I explored. The marsh went as far as the I could see, in every direction. I could hear strange sounding birds cawing in the trees. Frogs made high pitched ringing noises in the tall reeds. Sometimes I heard something splash in the water nearby, and it made me jump. It was an eerie, smelly place.

Through the trees and hanging moss, I could see the road close by. It was built up on top of a dirt levy so wagons and horses didn't have to fight through the mud to get across the marsh. I climbed up to the top of the levy and stood in the road, looking down both ways without seeing anyone. Something about this place gave me the creeps, like maybe something was watching me that I couldn't see.

I walked down the road for a few yards, swatting flies away from my face. Even though I was worn out, and worried about Sile, it was nice to have a few minutes to myself to think. I thought about the things I'd heard Sile say. Something about tampering with gods. I wondered what that meant, and what it had to do with him. What could he possibly have done that would make anyone want to kill him?

It was so quiet except for the birds and frogs, and that's when I heard Beckah scream. It almost made me jump out of my boots. My heart started to pound, and I started running as fast as I could through the mud and slop to get back to them. I hadn't let them out of my sight for more than a few minutes …

… But I was already too late.

There were six big men standing in our small clearing, and all of them were armed with swords and crossbows. But there was no way these guys were soldiers. They were wearing black cloaks, and mismatched pieces of armor. All of them looked filthy and sweaty, and they laughed at me when I stumbled into the clearing.

"That's it? That's the best yah got?" A man with a long curly beard had Beckah by her hair, and was holding a long dagger against her throat. He laughed at me and grinned with his crooked yellow teeth. "A halfbreed wearin the king's colors? Now that's a joke I never heard before!"

A few of the other men laughed again, and it made our dragons snarl. Nova and Mavrik were crouched together, hissing and showing their teeth as the men pointed crossbows at them.

"Let the kids go," Felix growled suddenly. He was standing with his back to the tree where he'd been sleeping earlier. Another man had a sword pointed at him, and Felix had his hands raised in the air. "You'll get a ransom for me, but you'd be wasting your time with them. A halfbreed and the daughter of a poor country knight don't go for much."

The bearded man cackled another gravelly, rasping laugh. "You think I'm interested in ransomin' any of you? Don't be stupid, boy."

"We don't have any money!" I yelled at him, feeling my face burn with fury. "We don't have anything for you to steal!"

When they all laughed at me again, I realized what they were. Slavers. I'd seen these kinds of people before. Filthy liars who captured anyone they could to be sold in the slave market. They weren't going to care who we were, or what we had; they would sell us off as workers for the mines, or worse.

"The halfbreed won't fetch much," one of the men pointed out. "He looks sickly. We'd be better off dumping him at one of the prison camps."

The bearded man seemed to agree. He pulled Beckah's hair and it made her whimper in pain. "We'll more than make up for the loss with her. A pretty young thing like this? There are plenty of pleasure houses in Halfax that'll pay twenty in solid gold for her. I bet no one's ever even kissed those soft lips of hers yet."

"Leave her alone!" My face burned. I was seeing red. Beckah was looking right at me with her big green eyes begging me to do something.

One of the slavers aimed a crossbow right at me, and gave me an evil smirk like he would shoot me just for fun. It made Mavrik roar with rage, snapping his teeth and making the guys pointing their crossbows at him a little nervous.

"Call off the dragons, halfbreed," the bearded man commanded. He was looking right at me. "And I won't cut her throat open right here."

I wanted to tell Mavrik to burn them all to dust. The arrows from the crossbow wouldn't have hurt him much, not with his thick scales to protect him. But I wasn't going to risk Beckah's life. I couldn't risk her being burned along with them.

"Go, Mavrik." I told him. My dragon looked at me like he couldn't believe I was agreeing. His yellow eyes narrowed, and he hissed again in defiance. "It's all right. I'll be fine. Just go. Take Nova with you."

Mavrik didn't like it, but he obeyed. He growled and glared at them as he retreated backwards into the marsh. Nova followed, and after a few minutes, I could hear their thundering wing beats as they took off into the sky.

"Tie 'em up, boys! And bring the wagon around!" The bearded man bellowed, throwing Beckah down into the mud at his feet. She hit the ground hard, and I saw her arms shaking as she tried to sit back up.

Felix cursed and fought them until a slaver kneed him hard in the gut, making him fall to his knees and groan. He couldn't fight anymore after that, and they tied his hands behind his back with ropes. They tied Beckah up, too, and then they started after me.

I backed up a few paces, tripping over my own feet in the mud. I could try to run, but there was no way I could outrun their arrows. Besides, I wasn't going to abandon my friends like that. I raised my hands in surrender, and went down on my knees before I gave any one of those slavers the satisfaction of getting to kick or punch me, too. They tied my wrists behind my back so tightly I could feel the circulation being cut off immediately.

The slavers were traveling in a big group of ten or so armed men. The bearded man, who they called Grothar, was obviously in charge. He ordered us to be taken up to the road, and we stood there waiting with slavers guarding us on all sides while two wagons pulled by a team of horses galloped toward us. I still didn't know how they'd found us, but that was the least of my worries now.

The wagons stopped right in front of us, and I got my first good look at the slave caravan. Both the wagons were made of solid black metal, with only one long, narrow window cut into the top of the door. It was barred, so no one could escape through it.

We came to the first wagon, and Grothar started barking out orders to his men. "Hurry it up, boys! I don't pay you to stand around runnin your mouths!"

Grothar opened the door to the first wagon with a big ring of keys he wore clipped to his sword belt. The slavers shoved Beckah into it. The inside of the wagon was totally dark, so I couldn't see into it, but I heard the panicked cries of other girls inside. It made fury boil in the pit of my stomach. There was nothing I could do as they slammed the door and locked it again.

Felix and I were tossed into the second wagon. It was just the same as the first, except there were men and boys in it instead of girls. It smelled like rotten hay and sweat, and I could hear other people moving around close by. When Grothar shut the door, it was pitch black, and the wagon groaned and rattled as it started moving again.

"Jaevid?" I heard Felix wheezing my name. He must have still been in pain from the blow he'd taken because his voice was raspy and faint. "Call Mavrik back like you did before! Get him to burn these guys to ash!"

I was struggling to sit up with my arms tied. I couldn't even move without bumping into someone close to me in the dark. It was terrifying, and it made it impossible think about anything except how afraid I was. I tried to find that same kind of calm I'd had before, to get that knot of heat back in my chest. But I couldn't focus at all. It was like my fear was jumbling my thoughts, making me confused. I worried about where we were going, I worried about Sile, about Beckah, and how we were going to get out of this mess.

Of all the bad things that might ever happen to me in my life, going to a prison camp was the worst possible option. Most gray elves got to live in the ghettos, but if they ever broke any rules or were caught doing anything illegal, they were put in shackles, loaded into wagons just like this one, and shipped off to the prison camps.

Not one of them was ever heard from again. I had seen it happen before. Mothers and fathers torn from their shacks, separated from their children. Anyone who tried to help them ran the risk of being shipped off, too. Those images played through my mind over and over, and I was so afraid that I couldn't breathe.

"I-I can't," I stammered and choked. "Felix ... what's going to happen to us?! I can't go to a prison camp! Felix, p-please! They'll kill me in there!" Tears were starting to well up in my eyes, and my chest felt tight. I was fighting for every breath.

Through my fear and panic, Felix's voice reached out to me in the darkness. He still sounded hoarse, but he was totally calm. "Jaevid, listen to me. You have to calm down right now. You're a dragonrider. You can beat this. But you can't let yourself surrender to fear. So pull yourself together. It's time to man up. You're not a kid anymore."

I could hear the whispering of other voices around us. There were at least a dozen other people in the back of the wagon, but all I could see of them was faint shadows and occasionally the gleam of their eyes. They were like ghosts in the darkness.

I shut my eyes to block them out, and tried to concentrate on my breathing. Felix was right. I had to pull myself together. Beckah needed me. Sile needed me.

Dragonrider or not, I couldn't let this be the end. I had to survive.

"You still with me?" Felix asked.

"Y-yeah. Yeah. I'm fine." I answered.

"Good." His voice was getting a little clearer and stronger. "Because I have a plan."

seventeen

I was smaller and more flexible, so I started working my way out of the ropes first. The slavers had tied me up tight, but I was able to curl my legs up to my chest and slip my arms under my feet. Once I had my hands in front of me, it was much easier to move around. My eyes were getting used to the small amount of light that trickled in from the narrow window at the top of the door, and I could see Felix sitting nearby.

"I've got it." I whispered to him. I didn't want to run the risk of the slavers outside hearing me. "Hurry up and turn around."

He scooted closer and sat with his back to me. I had to feel around in the dark to find the ropes tied around his wrists, which was awkward since my hands were still tied together, too. I started untying him, and when I got the ropes loose, Felix was able to work them off himself. I heard him let out a loud sigh of relief.

While he untied the ropes on my wrists, Felix was looking around like he was plotting. I had no idea what he was going to do. Things didn't look so good from where I was sitting. We were outnumbered, locked in what was basically a metal box on wheels, and neither of us had a weapon.

"F-Felix?" A familiar voice whispered from the dark. It startled me because even though I couldn't see him, I knew who it was immediately. Lyon Cromwell was tied up in a corner of the wagon with his wrists and ankles tied up. While I couldn't be sure in the faint light, it looked almost like he had a black eye.

"Lyon?" I had to ask because I thought maybe my mind was just playing tricks on me. Why would he be in the back of a slaver's wagon?

"It's really you!" His voice was shaking, and he started sobbing. "Please, you have to get me out of here. Don't leave me here!"

Felix untied my hands and went to start doing the same for Lyon. I followed, but I kept my distance. After all, I hadn't had very good experiences with Lyon in the past. In fact, he had tried to beat me to death both times.

"You idiot," Felix growled at him as he pulled at the ropes. "How did you wind up in here?"

Lyon was sobbing hysterically. "H-he promised me I'd get promoted straight to captain!" I could barely understand him as he sniffled. "But he tricked me! They all lied!"

"Who?" I dared to ask.

He shuddered. "The king's Lord General. He came to me while we were at Blybrig, before training ever started. He said if I did what he told me, if I cooperated, he'd make sure I was promoted to captain straight out of the academy."

"You really are an idiot," Felix growled as he finished untying him. "You fell for that?"

"He's the Lord General! I had no reason not to trust him!" Lyon barked back defensively.

"Why is he trying to kill Lieutenant Derrick?" I tried to cut off their argument before it got started. After all, it wasn't like we had a lot of time. "And where are they taking us?"

"I-I don't know the details. At first, he just wanted me to sabotage Lieutenant Derrick's saddle. Hey wanted me to make sure that ... well, you know. But he came to me again before we left for Duke Brinton's. That time he just wanted me to lure Lieutenant Derrick out of the ballroom. Those guardsmen in masks jumped us as soon as we were alone." Lyon stammered and sniffled. He sat up and started rubbing his wrists. I could see him a little better when he leaned into the light from the window. He definitely had a big, shiny black eye.

"You don't know anything about why they'd want to kill a decorated, Seasoned Lieutenant like that?" Felix growled at him threateningly. "That didn't sound the slightest bit suspicious to you?"

Lyon actually looked a little afraid of him. "I don't know why, I swear! They didn't tell me anything. But I overheard the Lord General talking to those guardsmen from the king. They were saying something about a stone. They called it the god stone."

Felix and I glanced at each other. I had no idea what a god stone was, and I got the feeling he didn't either. But this couldn't be good—not if it was worth killing over.

"Do you know where they're taking us?" I asked him again.

Lyon started wiping his nose, but he was beginning to pull himself together. "The prison camp outside of Halfax, I think. I heard some of the slavers talking about it."

Felix grabbed the front of his tunic suddenly. It surprised me, and it made Lyon tremble and throw his hands up in surrender.

"This is all your fault, you little worm," Felix growled

through his teeth. "Where is Lieutenant Derrick? Where did they take him? You better start talking, or so help me, I'll make both your eyes black!"

"Felix!" I touched his shoulder hesitantly. I was kind of afraid he'd hit me too, just out of blind fury. "Let him go. Just calm down. This isn't going to help." I hoped Lyon didn't change his opinion of me too much, just because I was saving his neck now. If Felix still wanted to beat him up after this was over, I wasn't sure I'd be so quick to stop him.

As soon as Felix let him go, Lyon started backing away from us frantically. His eyes were wide, and he looked terrified. "They separated us," he started to explain. "I saw them put Lieutenant Derrick in the back of another wagon. We only stopped once, outside the marsh. I guess they must have seen you guys flying over, because they started shouting orders and split up the caravan. The Lord General and the king's guardsmen took the lieutenant the long way around the marsh."

Felix cursed. It was a big mess, but at least now we knew how the slavers had found us in the first place. They'd probably been lying in wait for us to land. "Well, at least we're going in the right direction." He snorted.

I wasn't nearly as glad about that as he was. I didn't care which direction we were going—all I wanted to do was get out of this wagon. "So what's your plan for getting out of here? There's only one door, and it's locked from the outside."

Felix shot me a dangerous look. It made me wonder if he was going to punch me in the face, too. "You get to work on calling Mavrik back. You did it once before, you can do it again. You have to. Because if I have to go with my fallback plan, it's basically guaranteed to get all or most of us killed in the process." I swallowed hard when he turned away again. "Lyon, help me cut loose the rest of the prisoners."

Lyon hesitated. "But … they're gray elves."

He was right about that. There were three other men in the back of the wagon, and all of them were gray elves. They were just staring at us with their diamond-colored eyes as big as saucers. They didn't say a word, and I knew that was because they were probably terrified of Felix and Lyon. One of them was elderly, his skin sunken against his cheekbones, and another looked like he was about Sile's age. The last seemed to be about Felix's age, and he just kept staring right at me.

"So?" Felix challenged. I saw him turn on Lyon, using the fact that he was bigger and definitely stronger to dare him to say something about it. "You see anyone else in here who can help us?"

Lyon did not look happy. I could see the disgust on his face as he went to help Felix untie the other prisoners.

I could also see how afraid the gray elves were. They were terrified, and began pleading with us in the garbled elven language not to hurt them.

"Can't you get the halfbreed to tell them to shut up? They're going to give us away if they keep jabbering on like this." Lyon grumbled.

Felix didn't get a change to jump to my defense. I beat him to it. "I don't speak elven," I snapped at him.

Even Felix looked surprised about that. The way they were both looking at me in stunned silence made me blush until the tips of my pointed ears burned.

"At least, not very well anymore," I clarified. After all, I could understand it. I had spoken it once, when I lived with my mother, but that seemed like such a long time ago. "My father didn't allow it. I haven't spoken it in years. I don't remember much."

The silence was awkward. Now the gray elves were staring at me, too. They probably hadn't understood anything I'd said, but I knew why they were staring at me. I was a halfbreed, after all. They didn't like my kind, either.

"Just get to work." Felix commanded.

I didn't argue. I sat on the floor of the wagon, and tried to get my mind to be quiet like it had been before. I tried to push away the fear, and find that knot of warmth in my chest that sent chills over my body like a cold shiver. I focused so hard that sweat started to run down my forehead and get into my eyes. I concentrated as hard as I could, but the jarring motion of the wagon interrupted my thoughts. It made me wonder if Beckah was okay, and worry about if we would even be able to get to Sile in time now. As easy as it would have been to just blame Lyon for everything, I didn't. It was the Lord General, the supreme leader of all the dragonriders in the kingdom, who had started this. It was his fault.

I started to get frustrated with myself. I was getting angry, and my hands shook as I clenched them into fists. "*Just get me out!*" I yelled, slamming my fists down onto the floor of the wagon. It made a loud metallic thump.

Just like last time, nothing happened at first. Minutes passed, and Lyon was staring at me like I was out of my mind. Felix just looked worried, but the second he opened his mouth to say something to me … there was an earth-shaking rumble from underneath the wagon.

All of a sudden, the wagon stopped. Outside, I could hear the sounds of men yelling and running past. My heart pounded in my ears as I strained to hear Mavrik's thundering roar coming to our rescue.

I did hear a roar. It was a bellow so deep that it made the wagon shudder, and the horses outside began to whinny in terror. It definitely wasn't Mavrik or Nova.

"What was that?" Lyon whispered shakily.

Felix was still staring at me with eyes wide and afraid. "Not a dragon," he whispered back. "Jae … what did you bring here?!"

I had no answer. I didn't know. The earth shook again, and the bellowing roar shook the wagon again. The gray elves started praying in frantic voices, and clawing at the walls of the wagon. We were stuck inside, only able to listen as men shouted and fought outside. I could hear arrows from crossbows pinging against the side of the wagon.

Felix covered his nose with his hand, and he frowned hard. "What is that smell?"

I smelled it, too. It reminded me of the silt mud from the marsh; the reeking stench of old rotting plant life. It was putrid, and it made my eyes water.

Suddenly the back half of the wagon blew open. Shards of metal flew, and I was ripped right off my knees and sent flying out into the sunlight. I bounced off the ground like a stone off the surface of a pond, and when I finally landed, I couldn't catch my breath. I gasped and wheezed, looking up through the spray of mud and the chaos of slavers running back and forth.

What I saw made my jaw drop. I was too afraid to move. Never in my life had I even heard of something like this before, but there it was—a massive, incredibly huge, utterly giant turtle.

It was as tall as four horses stacked on top of each other, with massive claws on its feet and a big, diamond-shaped head. Its shell was covered in jagged, sharp spines, and there was old moss and vines hanging off it. When it snapped its jaws at the slavers, its neck shot out like a snake's strike, and I saw it split shields in half like crackers. It was fast, huge, and covered in thick plated scales. None of the slavers' arrows even pierced it, but they kept firing anyway.

"Gods and Fates!" I heard Felix shout in horror. He was running toward me, but he didn't take his eyes off the giant turtle. "Jaevid, why would you bring something like that here?!"

Lyon was right behind him, running for his life and screaming, "It's a paludix turtle!"

I staggered to my feet. "Try to find a weapon," I yelled at Felix over the chaos. "I'm going after Beckah!"

Immediately, I started to search the chaos for the other wagon. My heart hit the back of my throat hard when I finally saw it. The horses pulling it had spooked and charged right off the levy into the swamp. They were panicking in the deep mud, and the wagon was turned over on its side. I could see hands sticking out of the barred rear window, and hear the women inside crying for help.

I ran like mad straight for the toppled wagon, skidded

down the steep side of the levy, and splashed into the waist-deep muck. By the time I got to the back door of the wagon, adrenaline was pumping through my veins like fire.

"Beckah!" I screamed her name at the top of my lungs.

From inside the wagon, I heard her answer. "Jaevid!"

She was alive, and for a moment I saw her face through the narrow window. She stuck a hand out through the bars, and I grabbed it. "I'll get you out!"

I had no idea how I was going to keep that promise. The door was still locked with a big iron padlock, and about the time I thought to look back for Grothar and his ring of keys ... I saw his legs disappear down the paludix turtle's throat.

I pulled at the lock, yanking at it futilely and trying to think of some other way to get the door open. I needed something to pry the lock off, something strong and narrow enough to fit through the loop in the padlock. I waded through the mud as fast as I could, and climbed up into the driver's seat of the wagon that was tilted on its side. I had hitched up Ulric's horse and wagon plenty of times. I knew where all the parts and pieces should be, so as soon as my hand hit the big iron pin that connected the horse harnesses to the wagon, I yanked it out. The horses whinnied in triumph, and began to gallop away through the swamp.

The pin was perfect. It was made of iron, long and narrow just like a big stake, and I carried it back to start trying to pry the lock off. It probably would have worked for anyone else right away. But I wasn't big enough. I couldn't get enough strength against it to crack the lock. I fought and struggled, slipping in the mud and cursing out loud.

I was about to give up and try something else, when two sets of bigger hands grabbed the iron pin right next to mine. I was surprised to see Felix and the younger gray elf boy standing beside me. They pushed with me, putting all our strength against the lock. With a sudden lurch and a loud crack, the lock popped off, and Felix pulled the door open.

Four gray elf women came rushing out, tripping over their skirts in the deep mud. I searched for Beckah in the crowd, and finally found her still crouched in the back of the wagon. She had a little girl in her arms, a gray elf toddler who was crying and clinging to her desperately.

"Come on!" Felix shouted at her.

Beckah looked at him with fury in her eyes. "I won't leave her!" She was not very big herself, and she could barely carry the toddler much less run with her.

Before anyone else could speak, the gray elf boy that had been helping us with the door rushed in and took the child from Beckah. I heard him muttering under his breath, trying to comfort the frightened little girl. I couldn't understand much of what he said, but I did recognize a few words: my sister.

Beckah came out willingly then. She threw her arms around my waist and squeezed me so hard I couldn't breathe. I was so relieved to see her, to have her back in one piece, that I hugged her back as hard as I could.

"What are you waiting for?!" Lyon shouted down at us from the top of the levy. "We have to get out of here!"

The slavers were so caught up in their battle with the massive swamp turtle that they didn't even notice all their prisoners running free. We ran through the marsh, and the gray elves ran with us, trying to get as far away from the slavers and the giant turtle as we could. The sounds of the battle started to fade into the background until all I could hear was our footsteps sloshing in the mud, the sound of the frogs, and my own panting.

We didn't stop or slow down until it was dark. When we finally came to a patch of dry ground, one by one we all collapsed to sit down and catch our breath. We were a muddy, soggy, exhausted mess. But we were alive, and right then, that's all I cared about.

The gray elves all grouped together, leaving Felix, Beckah, Lyon and I to sit off to ourselves. They hugged one another and spoke in hushed voices. I didn't try to eavesdrop on them; I could see the relief and happiness on their faces. They were free, for now.

"I can't believe it," Lyon panted. He was lying on his back with his arms and legs sprawled out. "First I get sold to slavers by the Lord General, then nearly devoured by an extinct species."

I glanced at Felix, and the look on my friend's face was enough to give me cold chills. His eyes were focused on me, but they were haunted. There was something about his expression that made me feel like he really was afraid of me now. "The great paludix turtle has been extinct for hundreds of years." He muttered in a hushed voice. "Or at least, we thought it was."

Lyon raised his head up to shoot me an accusing glare. "What exactly did you do, halfbreed?"

"It must have been in hiding for decades." Felix spoke up in my defense. Or at least, that's what I thought until he added, "Until you called it out."

Now I felt cornered. Everyone except Beckah was looking at me like I was some kind of monster—like I had done something terrible. I knew why, of course. Humans had always suspected gray elves of using wicked magic and mischievous spells to manipulate people. They'd even called my mother a witch because of the way she could make the plants grow when she was alive. I didn't know if what I could do—calling out to animals with my thoughts—even qualified as something magical at all. But it was enough to get some accusing, disgusted looks from my so-called friends.

"I only did what you told me to," I reminded Felix angrily. I couldn't help it. It felt like he was turning on me, which was the last thing I expected. "How was I supposed to know that thing would hear me?"

I got up and stormed away from them, going to sit on the edge of our dry little patch of land by myself. I just couldn't stand to be around him when he was looking at me that way. It was one thing for Lyon to treat me like a traitor, but Felix was supposed to be my friend.

For a long time, I just sat there and watched the sun set over the marsh. The crickets and frogs sang in the tall reeds. Fireflies started blinking in the dark like warm orange spots of light. I took the necklace my mother had given me out from under my shirt, feeling the smooth polished bone while I thought about her. It had been a long time since I'd seen other gray elves, and now it was starting to catch up to me. It made me miss my mother. She was the one person in the world who had loved me unconditionally.

I didn't say anything when Beckah suddenly came over. She sat down beside me with her legs crossed under her stained blue dress. For a few minutes we just sat there and didn't say anything, even though I could tell there was something she wanted to say.

"What's that?" She pointed to my necklace.

I glanced down at it, running my thumb over the smooth white pendant. "My mother gave it to me before she died." I grumbled. I didn't feel like talking at all, much less about my mother. It just made me miss her more.

"It's beautiful," she said in a quiet voice.

I started to feel bad. I was being cold to her, and none of this was her fault. She didn't deserve to be treated like that. I let out a heavy sigh, and gave up being mad at Felix. "She said it would protect me." I glanced over at Beckah, and tried to give her a convincing smile. "I guess it doesn't work very well."

Beckah smiled back at me. She had mud in her hair, all over her dress, and even smeared on her face. But her green eyes still shone brightly. "You made it into the academy to be a dragonrider. You jumped off the top of a tower at the duke's estate and lived. And now you saved us all from slavers, and a giant man-eating turtle. I think it works pretty well." She laughed a little.

I couldn't help but laugh, too. Maybe it did work, after all. "So, how did everyone in your wagon get out of the ropes?"

She smiled proudly. "My daddy does teach me a few things when he comes home. He didn't give me a magical necklace, but he taught me how to escape ropes and shackles when I was little. He made it like a game, you know? It was really fun. And it made my momma furious. He started teaching me how to shoot a bow, but momma put a stop to that. She said girls don't shoot bows."

I had underestimated her. She was a kid, sort of, but she was brave, and she was definitely a lot smarter than I was. "Your dad is a good man, Beckah," I told her. "No matter what else happens, you should know that."

"You are too, you know." She gave me a meaningful look. I could see on her face that this is what she'd really come over to talk to me about. "Whatever you did back there, I know you just wanted to help us. You're a good person. And if Felix and that other guy can't see that, well, then they're too dumb to be dragonriders anyway."

I blushed. "It's not because they're dumb, Beckah. It's because I'm a—"

"No, she's right." Felix butted in suddenly. It startled me, and I turned around to see him standing behind us with his arms crossed. He didn't look angry, or even wary of me anymore. In fact, he looked frustrated and embarrassed. "I'm sorry, Jae."

I was so surprised I couldn't even say anything back at first. All I could do was just nod at him a little and smile awkwardly. How could I not forgive him? Felix was my friend, and one of the best ones I'd ever had. If I lost him, I probably wouldn't last very long in the academy. The other fledglings would eat me alive and toss whatever was left to their dragons.

"It's okay," I told him. "This whole calling to animals thing is weird for me, too."

"Did your momma ever tell you anything about it?" Beckah looked worried. "Is it something all gray elves can do?"

I shook my head. "No, she never mentioned this. I've never even heard of it before."

"Well, whatever it is, we should probably keep it between us," Felix suggested. "It'd freak the instructors out."

I couldn't argue with that. He was definitely right. The last thing I needed was to give the instructors at Blybrig one more reason not to trust me. Until I figured this out, we had to keep it a secret. I couldn't use it unless it was absolutely necessary. If anyone else found out, at the very least it could get me kicked out of the academy.

"But what about that other guy?" Beckah cut a suspicious glance over to Lyon, who was still sprawled out on the ground.

Felix smirked, and started cracking his knuckles. "Leave Lyon to me."

eighteen

The gray elves were doing a lot better surviving in the marsh than we were. They built a small fire, and were sitting around it together roasting something that smelled amazing. I was already starving, and the smell of whatever they were cooking made my mouth water. It must have had the same effect on Felix because he was just sitting there, staring at them, with a miserable expression on his face.

"We should just demand that they give us a share," Lyon growled. "After all, we were the ones who did all the work."

"Yeah, sure." Felix rolled his eyes. "Why don't you go over there and tell them that yourself? Let us know how that goes."

"Send the halfbreed, then." Lyon bargained. He seemed determined not to use my name.

I shot him a glare. "They hate me just as much as you do, you know."

That seemed to surprise Lyon. "What? But you're—"

I cut him off before he could finish. "—half human. They don't like me for the same reasons you don't."

"I'll go," Beckah offered. She was licking her lips hungrily. It might have actually worked to send the most innocent and vulnerable of our group to beg for scraps, but I wasn't about to let Beckah risk herself on that chance. I didn't know the gray elves might do.

About the time Felix and Lyon started arguing over who should go, I noticed that the younger gray elf man from before was walking our way. He didn't look much older than Felix, but his hair was already that shining silver color. The gray elves were all born with black hair that turned silver once they finally hit puberty, so he had to be at least eighteen for his hair to already look like that.

He stood awkwardly on the edge of our pitiful excuse for a camp, which was basically just the four of us sitting in a circle, holding something that was wrapped up in charred leaves. His diamond-colored eyes flicked from one of us to the other, and he finally started to speak. Of course, he didn't speak the human language, and when he talked he looked right at me like he expected me to understand him.

I did understand some of what he said. He told us his name was Kiran, and then he offered what he had in his hands. It was roasted roots that they had dug up out of the earth, wrapped in damp leaves, and baked in their fire. The smell was fantastic, even for something that came out of this smelly marsh.

"These are gifts for us," I translated, giving Felix a hesitant look. "For helping them, I guess." The gray elf language was very complex and I hadn't heard it, much less spoken it in years.

Felix smiled tiredly at him, and got up to take the food from him. Beckah and Lyon did the same, while Kiran kept eyeing them warily. It was like he half-expected a sneak attack.

When I got up to take some of the food from him, Kiran's expression went from uncomfortable to total disgust. He looked me over from head to toe, like everyone did, and I saw his nose wrinkle. The gray elves didn't want me anywhere near them, just like the humans. I was both, and I was neither.

He didn't say a word to me as I took the food from his hands. I began to turn away, ready to go sit with my friends, until I saw his eyes go straight to the necklace my mother had given me. I'd forgotten to tuck it back under my shirt.

"Where did you get that?" he snapped at me in the elven language. He was pointing at my necklace.

I glanced down at it before tucking it back under my shirt collar. I didn't want him to get any ideas about taking it. "A gift." I answered. I spoke to him in English because I had a sneaking suspicion he could, too. He was young enough that he'd probably been born in an elven ghetto, just like me.

Kiran's lip twitched and his eyes narrowed. "Who gave it to you?" he demanded—in English this time.

I glared at him with as much courage as I could muster. "It's none of your business."

He got a mean smirk on his lips that made me nervous. Fortunately, Felix was sitting not too far away, and I could see him watching us out of the corner of my eye.

"I know that mark," Kiran said as he pointed to the king's eagle stitched onto my tunic. "You wear the clothes of the human warriors, but you're too young to even remember who started this war." The way he said it made it sound like an insult.

As much as I just wanted to turn my back to him and walk away, something about the way he talked down to me really got on my nerves. I was used to being treated that way by humans, but usually gray elves just ignored me like I didn't exist. Kiran was the first one to go out of his way to pick on me. If my mom had been alive, she would have smacked him across the face. But me? Well, I had had enough of being pushed around for one day.

"I don't care who started the war," I told him. "And I don't care who wins it."

Kiran gave me a funny look, like that wasn't the answer he'd expected. "Why do you fight with them, caenu?"

I didn't have a good answer for that, so I just glared at him for a few seconds and then looked away. It was a difficult question to even think about. I hadn't really considered the idea that eventually I would be on the battlefield with a sword in my hand, trying to kill gray elves like Kiran. And they would be trying to kill me, too.

When I didn't reply, Kiran went back to his own circle around the campfire with the other gray elves. I looked at the food in my hand, and felt uneasy. I knew the gray elves had a social custom that demanded all debts be paid. So this must have been their way of repaying us for letting them all free, even if that had only been a side effect of our own escape.

Lyon was eyeing his roasted potato skeptically. "What if this is poisonous? How do we know they aren't trying to kill us?"

Beckah glared at him. "Don't be stupid. Of course it isn't poisonous."

He glared back, though he seemed a little stunned that a kid was talking back to him like that. "How do you know?" he challenged.

"Because they're eating it, too," she replied with a mouthful of potato.

We all looked over at the same time to stare at the gray elves. They were cozy, sitting close to their fire while they shared their own roasted potatoes. Beckah was right, and I was willing to chance it for the sake of my cramping hunger pains.

"What does caenu mean?" Felix asked as I sat down beside him and started unwrapping my own ration. "That elf, I heard him call you that. What does it mean?"

I was really rusty when it came to speaking the gray elf language, but there were a few words that stuck into my mind like thorns. Those were words I'd come to hate; words I could never forget. Caenu was one of them.

I just focused on eating my piping hot potato while I answered because I didn't want to see the look on his face. "It's what the gray elves call halfbreeds." I tried to sound as matter of fact about that as I could. I didn't want him to know how much it bothered me. "It means 'filth' in their language."

I could feel Felix's eyes on me for a long time. Maybe it had never really occurred to him that when I said the gray elves hated me as much as most humans did ... I really meant it. They didn't want me around them, either. My mother had been the exception. She had loved me. But I knew better than to hope I'd get that kind of reception from the rest of her kin.

"He was asking you about the war, wasn't he?" Felix questioned me again. "He was asking you why you want to fight with humans instead of elves?"

I swallowed hard and finally dared to meet his eyes. "Yeah."

His eyes narrowed some, and I saw his jaw tense. "And you really don't care who wins this war?"

Again, that question crept up on me and stunned me. I'd answered Kiran before without really thinking about it, and now that I had a chance to really mull it over, I realized my answer wasn't going to change. "No, I don't."

"How can you say that?" Felix sounded worried, maybe even a little insulted.

I shrugged and took another bite of potato. "Because it doesn't matter to me. Neither side wants me, and no matter who wins, that probably won't ever change. I'll always be hated by both humans and elves because of what I am. So why would I want to fight for them?"

"So you're just fighting for the sake of having a job? Or so you won't have to go to a prison camp?" His brows were furrowed, and he was frowning at me hard.

"No that's not the reason," I corrected. "Well, maybe

it is *a* reason, but it's not the *main* reason."

"Then what is?"

I looked at Felix squarely in the eye. "I'm going to fight for you. You said it yourself, that we're in this together. We're partners, right? So I'll fight to watch your back. It's the same reason I'm out here trying to save Sile. There aren't very many people in the world who care what happens to me. You, Sile, Beckah, Katty, even Mavrik are pretty much the only ones. So I'll do what I can to protect you, even if that means fighting in a war that'll end up being a no-win situation for me either way. It's worth it."

Felix's expression wavered. I saw that he wanted to smile, but he didn't. There was sadness in his eyes, deep heavy sadness. He just nodded some before he went back to eating.

Even with warm food in my stomach and no strength in my body, it was hard to sleep. I had nightmares about giant turtles and slavers. Early the next morning, I woke up with my heart hammering because I thought I heard the sound of hoof beats. But we were alone—completely alone.

The gray elves were gone. All that was left of them were a few tracks in the mud, leading away across the marsh. They'd left us there to fend for ourselves, not that I was sad to see them go. Being around them was sometimes worse than being around humans.

What I'd mistaken for hoof beats started to get louder. When I realized what that sound actually was, I started shaking Beckah awake and yelling for Felix to get up. The sound got even louder and closer, and I heard the familiar bellow of Mavrik's roar from above the trees.

Seeing a flash of his blue scales and the sound of his roar made my heart soar. He'd come back for me. I certainly wouldn't have blamed him for just leaving me there to fend for myself, after the way I'd dismissed him before.

He and Nova were circling above us, looking for a good place to land. With so many trees growing so close together, there wasn't a place big enough for them. Suddenly, I got another one of those radical ideas.

"Come on, I'll give you a boost." I said as I pulled Beckah up to her feet. She was still rubbing the sleep from her eyes, blinking up at the sky. I don't think she really understood what I was doing until I was pushing her up toward the lowest hanging limb of a nearby tree.

"Are you crazy?" Lyon was awake and already protesting.

Felix just laughed, and started climbing up after me. "Better stay down here, Lyon. We wouldn't want you to risk hurting yourself just to follow us, would we?" The sarcasm in his voice made me laugh, too.

"You're not leaving me behind!" Lyon declared as he started climbing up the tree after us.

When I got to the top, to the very skinniest of the limbs that would hold my weight, I looked out across the marshland. I could see the tops of the trees for miles and miles around us. Far in the distance, I could see the mountains like ghostly blue shadows on the horizon.

Mavrik made a loud screeching noise as he swooped in low and circled around me. Now it was time for my plan. I got Beckah as close to me as I could to wrap an arm around her waist.

"You have to hang on to me," I told her.

She nodded and wrapped her arms around my neck. "I'm not afraid. I trust you."

When Mavrik came swooping low again, his powerful wings spread out wide, I gave him the hand signal for doing a roll. I wasn't sure he'd get it, I mean, we'd never really perfected his understanding of the hand signals we riders used in the air. But as he started to get dangerously close, he whipped over with his back facing down toward us.

I jumped straight up with all my might, reaching for the saddle handles. Not in a million years did I think I'd actually grab them. He was moving fast, like a streak of blue lightning. My timing had to be absolutely perfect.

And it was.

I grabbed the saddle handles, hanging on for dear life as we were suddenly snatched off the top of the tree. Mavrik rolled over, and I quickly got myself settled into the saddle with Beckah sitting right in front of me. We cruised over the tops of the trees, making a wide turn to go back and make sure Felix and Lyon were able to get on Nova.

I'm pretty sure Lyon was crying when they were finally sitting on Nova's back, him hugging Felix as he sat in the back of the saddle. Felix gave me a thumb's up, letting me know they were okay.

Take the lead, I signed to him. *We've got to get to Halfax before they do.*

Felix smirked, and I saw him lean down closer to Nova's neck. He put on the speed, and Nova shot forward like a brown and gold bullet. Mavrik roared at her, and I felt his body go tense and solid beneath the saddle. He beat his wings hard, and we went hurling forward with a new burst of speed.

Beckah reached to grab my hand, squeezing it until her knuckles were white.

"It's okay," I yelled to her over the rush of the wind. I thought she was afraid, but when I saw her face … I could see that she was smiling.

Her eyes were wide, and she was looking out across the trees that blurred past. She looked at me with a huge grin. "This is amazing!"

I smiled back at her, and brushed some of her hair away that was blowing into my eyes. I wasn't sure if I'd ever noticed before, but Beckah was really pretty—even if she did look a lot like her father. When she smiled at me like that, it made me blush.

Mavrik snapped his wings in sharp, quick beats that sent us bolting forward until we caught up to Nova. We kept our pace fast and our position as low to the ground as we dared. When we reached the other side of the marsh, I could see the royal city of Halfax far in the distance. I knew it right away because of the tall, swirling spires of the king's castle set back from the rest of the city against the side of a huge cliff. You could see the castle from just about anywhere in the city, even from the gray elf ghetto where I'd lived with my mother.

Beyond the city's outskirts and surrounding farmlands was the prison camp. I'd never actually seen it before, but I knew what it was right away. From the air, it looked like a dark patch on the horizon. It was a big complex surrounded by high, black stone walls. The stones for those walls had been mined from the volcanic cliffs along the coast, so they were rough, uneven, and nearly impossible to climb without cutting your hands and feet to shreds. On the tops of the walls, tar mixed with shards of broken glass had been spread over it to keep people from trying to escape.

The prison camp was built in a big diamond shape with eight watchtowers looking down at the prisoners inside. From where we were, it just looked liked a big tangled mess of scrap surrounding one dark crater in the middle. The crater must have been an abandoned quarry, with layers of rock carved away to the glaring sunlight.

Seeing it, even from a distance, made my stomach tangle into painful knots. Ending up in a place like that was my absolute worst fear. I didn't want to go anywhere near it. I wanted to turn Mavrik around and bolt in the opposite direction. But Sile might already be there, trapped in that horrible place. We had to save him. I had given Beckah my word that we would, and I was determined to keep that promise.

"We've got to find a way inside," Felix said as soon as he dismounted. "If we try to take them from the air, chances are, the dragonriders stationed at the castle will come after us, and we'll all be arrested before we even get a chance to find Sile, that is if the bowmen in the watchtowers don't shoot us down first. Being stealthy will give us our best chance."

We had landed in a big open wheat field outside Halfax, about three miles from the prison camp. From where we stood, we had a straight view of it. Smoke rose up from beyond its tall black gates, and I was beginning to feel sick with dread.

"Break into a prison camp?" Lyon scoffed. He crossed his arms, and sneered at the idea. "You're all crazy. I'm not going in there. As if we could even get past the guards in the first place."

"It's your fault Sile is in there in the first place," Felix reminded him with a threatening growl. "You're coming with us, one way or another."

The two were about to start arguing again, glaring at each other and squaring off. I could sense the tension rising, but I wasn't eager to jump in the middle and break them up. It wouldn't exactly hurt my feelings if Felix beat Lyon to a bloody pulp.

"Y-you did this?" Beckah stammered suddenly. "But you're a dragonrider too, right?"

I flinched. Felix and I exchanged a glance. We hadn't told her Lyon was the one responsible for her father's abduction. I wasn't sure how she as going to handle that news.

Beckah was looking up at him with wide eyes. At first, I thought she might start crying. I could see revelation come over her whole demeanor as she started piecing it together that there was a traitor in our midst. Lyon had betrayed her father, and the reasons why didn't really matter.

But Beckah didn't cry. Instead, she balled her hands into fists and started for him with violent intent blazing in her eyes. "You! You did this! You're a traitor!" She screamed at him. "What did my daddy ever do to you?! You … you selfish coward!"

I grabbed her by the shoulder before she could actually start hitting him, pulling her back and holding her while she kicked and fought to get away from me. I wasn't going to take the chance that Lyon wouldn't hit her back just because she was a girl.

Lyon was staring back at her, and his expression was difficult to read. If he could have felt any remorse for what he'd done, maybe he did in that moment. I didn't know Lyon well enough to be sure.

"I hope you die!" Beckah screamed at him. "You deserve to die!"

I put a hand over her mouth, holding her tight against my chest as she kept on fighting me. "Hush, Beckah. Don't say that." I told her as calmly as I knew how. I started forcing her to walk a few yards away with me. She needed to cool off.

"How can you defend him?!" She turned on me next, and I saw angry, frustrated tears starting to brim in her eyes. Her cheeks were dark red, and her whole body was trembling.

As soon as we were far enough away that Felix and Lyon wouldn't be able to hear us, I grabbed her as tightly as I could. I hugged her. I held her that way, even though she fought me at first.

"I'm not defending him. He'll have to pay for what he did. But right now isn't the time. Right now, we have to concentrate on saving your dad. That's what's most important." I tried to talk gently to her to calm her down. She was just a kid, and even if I wasn't that much older than her, I felt like it was my responsibility to help her understand. "So just take some deep breaths. I know you're angry. Just calm down."

I heard her start to cry, and she quit fighting me. She put her arms around my waist and hugged me back, hiding her face against my shoulder.

"I hate him, Jae!" She whimpered.

"I know." I patted her head awkwardly. I wasn't sure what else I was supposed to do. My experience in comforting girls was pretty limited. "I'm not all that wild about him, either. He's used my face as a doormat before, you know."

"You'll make sure he doesn't get away with this, right?" she asked, looking up at me with her chin trembling.

I had already made some steep promises to her—promises I wasn't sure I could keep. But I'd try. After all, she deserved the very best effort I could give.

I nodded, "I'll try."

That seemed to satisfy her, and she pushed away from me a little. "People like that, who betray their own kind, they don't deserve any kind of justice. We should just throw him in the prison camp and see how he likes it."

I frowned at her. "You know, that's exactly the reason humans and gray elves don't like me, Beckah. They both think I'm a traitor to my race."

I saw her expression fall. Her shoulders hunched up some like she was embarrassed, and she looked away uneasily. "That's not the same thing," she mumbled stubbornly.

I knew she was still upset, and most of what she said was just out of anger and frustration. But it still stung. "You can't just condemn someone, no matter what they've done. Everyone deserves justice, even traitors."

nineteen

I had a feeling Felix was going to get us all killed. We had given our dragons the signal to lay low and wait for us to come back, but that didn't make me feel any better as we snuck into a barn outside one of the little farmhouses nearby. It was a few hours after dark, and Felix had decided we needed to find some weaponry before we tried to get into the prison camp.

As Felix pushed the barn door open a crack and we all rushed inside, I started to get a queasy feeling. The moonlight filtered through the slats in the ceiling, revealing harvesting scythes, axes, and a whole collection of farm tools hanging on the walls of the barn. There were big clay jugs crowded against the walls, crates stacked to the rafters, and big sacks of grain and feed for horses. Felix went straight for a big hunting knife that was lying on a table that looked like it had been used for butchering and dressing game.

I picked up a sickle and held it awkwardly, wondering if I could actually hurt anyone other than myself with it. "Felix, how is this going to work?" I turned around to face him. "How can we fight the king's elite guards with farm tools?"

He was shoving an axe in Lyon's hands. But Lyon dropped it as soon as Felix looked away. "Better to have something than nothing at all," he answered. "Look, hopefully it won't even come to that. Quick, take off your cloak and shirt."

I watched him pick up an empty feed sack off the floor and start cutting holes in it until it looked suspiciously like a tunic. "What for?" I frowned as he handed it to me, and then started making another one for himself. I did as he told me, stripping away my mud-caked tunic and putting on the scratchy burlap sack.

"We need to blend in. If they see us in fledgling uniforms, they'll know right away who we are. You, Lyon, and I are going to sneak in first. Once we're inside, Beckah and the dragons are going to create a diversion for us. We'll cut Lieutenant Derrick loose in the chaos while Lyon is getting the main gate open, and hopefully the guards will be so distracted, they won't even notice us escaping." Felix explained. "Jae, you speak enough elven that we should at least be able to talk to the other prisoners and figure out where they're holding him."

It sounded good, but I was still confused about how we were actually going to get inside in the first place. He didn't explain that part, and I was sort of afraid to ask.

"How do we know they've even arrived yet?" Beckah was watching us, and she looked really nervous. Not that I could blame her. If everything went according to plan, she'd be the one being shot at by guards and hunted by the dragonriders from the castle. I didn't like it. I didn't want to put her in danger, much less imagine what Sile would do to me if she got hurt. But I also trusted Mavrik. I knew he wouldn't let anything happen to her.

Felix made himself a crude-looking tunic to match mine out of another empty feed sack, and put it on. Then he took the sickle I'd picked up, and a long coil of rope. "We don't," he answered sharply. "But we can't afford to wait. By now, Commander Rayken has realized we're missing from Blybrig. They'll be looking for us. And if we get caught, then there's no one left to help your dad. This is our one and only chance."

Beckah nodded, and I saw her swallow hard. Our eyes met, and I tried to show her a confident smile. "It'll be fine." I told her. "Don't worry. Mavrik is the fastest dragon in Blybrig. Nothing will be able to catch up with you."

"*You* quit worrying," she insisted stubbornly. "I can do this."

Felix stooped down to pick up one of the clay jugs on the floor, pulling the cork out of the top and making a face like it smelled bad. I could smell it too, even from a few feet away. They were jars full of lamp oil. He handed it to her, and gave her a serious look.

"You better be able to do it," he warned. "Because it's our lives on the line."

Outfitted with our makeshift farm tool weapons and empty grain sacks for tunics, Felix, Lyon, and I hunkered down in the shadows only a few hundred yards away from the huge black wall of the prison camp. Beckah was already with Nova and Mavrik, waiting for our signal to start her diversion. I'd given her the best crash-course in flying I could, showed her how to sit in the saddle, and felt like a complete jerk for leaving her like that. Felix had tied about a dozen of those clay jugs full of oil to Mavrik's saddle, going over the plan with her several times. She kept insisting she wasn't scared. At least that made one of us.

After creeping in as close as we dared, Felix, Lyon and I were laying flat on our stomachs, side by side on the ground, and watching through the tall grass. There was only one gate, just one way in and out of the prison camp, and it was heavily guarded. More armed guards stood at each of the eight watchtowers, looking down over the inside and outside of the walls. Even more of them marched around the wall to keep watch for people trying to escape from inside.

"It looks like the perimeter patrols are set about five minutes apart," Felix whispered. "That doesn't give us much time to climb the wall."

"We'll have to do it one at a time, then. That's going to take too long. They might see us." I frowned over at him, hoping he had a better idea.

"There's no other choice. We'll just have to go as fast as possible." Felix reached to pull the bundle of rope and sickle out from where he'd tucked them in his belt. He started to tie one end of the rope to the sickle, like a makeshift hook and line we'd be able to use for climbing up the wall. "I'll go first, then you, Jae. After Lyon comes up last, we'll split up and then give Beckah the signal."

When the next guard walked past, we waited a few seconds. It was long enough that I glanced at Felix, wondering if he'd lost his nerve. But suddenly he took off, sprinting toward the wall and swinging the rope and sickle over his head like a lasso.

The wall was about two storeys tall. If he didn't hook the top on the first try, he might not have enough time to climb up before the next guard came by. He swung the rope harder and harder, and finally let it go, sending the sickle howling through the air and clattering against the stone. The sickle cracked against the shards of glass on top of the wall, scraped, and finally snagged with a loud crunch. It made me cringe. Someone definitely could have heard that.

We all waited, and I held my breath. But no one came. The guards hadn't heard us. Felix started reeling in the rope as fast as he could, giving it a few hard tugs before finally leaning his weight into it. When it held fast, he turned around and gave us a quick thumb's up. So far, so good.

He started to climb, using the side of the wall as leverage while he scaled the rope. Just as the last few inches of his boots disappeared up into the dark, the next guard came strolling by on patrol. I held my breath again, waiting to see if the guard would notice anything suspicious.

The guard walked past without even stopping, and all of a sudden it was my turn to climb. My heart was hammering. My hands were sweaty. I was petrified. But I set my jaw, balled my fists, and didn't give myself a single second to hesitate.

I bolted toward the wall, feeling around in the darkness for the rope. When I found it, I gave a tug.

From somewhere above me in the dark, I felt Felix tug back. The coast was clear, so I started to climb.

I didn't dare look back to see if the next guard was coming. I just tried not to think about that. The climb was a lot further up than I'd thought. From the ground, it had looked pretty high, but by the time I got to the top of the wall, I was sweating and heaving for breath. Felix grabbed my arms when I got within reach, and hauled me up the last few feet. The top of the wall was slathered in tar mixed with shards of glass, but Felix had spread out his cloak to keep us from getting cut up. He made sure I was steady before he gave me a pat on the back.

Next, it was Lyon's turn. Felix got himself braced, holding the end of the rope that was hooked to the top of the wall, just for good measure. And we waited.

Minutes passed. Two guards walked by down below, and I held my breath each time, expecting to see Lyon come sprinting up to the wall to start his own climb. Maybe it was just taking him longer to work up the nerve. But he didn't come, and it was too dark to see where we'd been hiding in the grass before.

A few more minutes passed, then another guard, and Felix cursed. "That little worm! He ditched us!"

I was stunned. Lyon hadn't exactly been a friend of ours—more like an enemy that was stuck with us for survival purposes—but this? This was twice he'd betrayed the dragonriders, twice he'd proven to be nothing but a lying coward. I cursed, too. Lyon was supposed to be the one who opened the gate to let us out once Beckah and the dragons stirred things up as a distraction. Now we were short one set of hands.

"We can't wait any longer," Felix growled under his breath as he reeled the rope in. "We'll just have to find some other way to escape. Maybe we can climb back down."

Felix had dismissed that idea originally because of the arrows that were sure to be flying in the chaos. One of us could get shot. I knew if he was considering that as our best option now, then we were in real trouble.

"You go," I told him. "Go get ready to open the gate. I'll get Sile."

His eyes got wide. "Jae, you can't go by yourself. What if something happens? What if you need me?"

"You said yourself that I've got the better shot at finding him. I'm the only one who can speak elven and talk to the prisoners." I held out my hand for him to shake. Something in my gut told me this might be the last time we ever saw each other. "You know this is the only way."

I could barely see Felix under the starlight as he looked down at my hand, and instead of shaking it, he took the big hunting knife he'd stolen from the barn and put it in my palm. "Yeah, I know. Just … try not to get killed." He clapped a hand against my shoulder roughly. "And remember, once the fire starts we only have a few minutes. Don't be late."

While Felix fixed the rope and makeshift hook so we could climb down the other side of the wall, I tucked the knife into my belt, making sure it was hidden under my scratchy burlap tunic. He let me climb down first. My head was spinning with fear as I repelled over the steep, jagged black stone. I prayed over and over that the guards wouldn't see me. And none of them did.

When my feet hit the ground, I looked around to get my bearings. It was dark, but the torches burning the watchtowers gave off just enough light that I could see the faint silhouettes of the buildings all around. They weren't really buildings, though. More like shacks made out of pieces of garbage for prisoners to live in.

Everything was eerily quiet and still, except for Felix's boots scraping off the stone from over head. He climbed down quickly, left the rope where it was, and hurried over to crouch down with me in the shadow of a nearby shack. My heart was pounding in my ears as I strained to see through the gloom. As my eyes adjusted, I could make out how all the garbage-made shacks surrounded the big crater in the middle of the prison camp. There were carved dirt stairwells leading down into the crater, and huge wheelbarrows that would take four or five people to move parked along the rim.

The inside of the prison camp smelled disgusting. It was like a mixture of filth, rotting flesh, and smoke that reeked like burning hair. There was also something in the air that left a mineral taste in my mouth. It was bitter, and made me want to spit.

"It's a salt mine," Felix whispered. "Can you taste it?"

"Yeah, but what's that smell?" I whispered back.

He just frowned darkly and pointed at the crater. "I'm not sure, but it's coming from in there. I don't like it, Jae. Something's not right."

Suddenly there was a metallic-sounding boom from the gate, and Felix and I tripped all over each other as we scrambled to hide. We ducked into a narrow crevice between two shacks, huddling in the dark and watching as the gate began to open.

The gate really was enormous, it was as tall as the walls, and made out of wood and iron. The only way to open it was by operating a crank in the heavily guarded tower. Just looking at it, I wondered if we really could pull this off. Strong as he was, I wasn't sure Felix could even open it by himself.

The massive gate creaked and groaned as it opened. Horse hooves clattered in the dark. Out of the gloom, a wagon appeared and came to a halt inside the prison camp. It looked just like the slave wagon we'd been trapped in before, made out of solid metal, and pulled by a team of black horses. My breath caught in my lungs, and it felt like I had swallowed something hard that was stuck in my throat. Sitting on the driving seat, still wearing those white masks, were two of the elite guards from the king.

My hand went to the knife hidden under my tunic, and I gripped the hilt tightly. Even though I couldn't see him, I knew that Sile was in that wagon. He just had to be. That is, if Lyon had been telling us the truth. A wave of nausea hit me when I realized just how much was riding on our assumption that Lyon hadn't been playing us the entire time.

As I watched the gate begin to roll closed again, it felt like someone was slowly choking me. It was like watching my freedom slip through my fingers, leaving Felix and me trapped in this horrible place. I wondered if that would be my last glimpse of the outside world beyond these prison walls.

Then, something else distracted me completely.

From overhead, I heard another sound like the deep, thunderous concussion of wing beats. But I knew this sound right away—it was the drumming of dragon wing beats in the air. Only this time, they sounded larger than any dragon I'd ever heard flying before.

The dragon was as black as the dark side of the moon, so the only way I knew it had landed was because I felt the earth rumble under my boots with the impact. I could see the shadows cast over its gleaming scales by the torchlight and the faint silver glow of the moon. It was a monster that looked like something from a nightmare. It was twice the size of Mavrik, with two red eyes that gleamed against the night like smoldering coals.

"Gods and Fates," Felix gasped. I saw his eyes look up as an enormous dark shape descended from the night sky. "It's Icarus."

"Who?" I didn't recognize the name, but I could see the horror and fear on his face.

"He's the Lord General's dragon. A king drake," Felix answered, and I could hear his voice quivering with fear. "When a dragon lives to be over a hundred years old, it becomes a king drake or grand queen. They're the largest and most powerful dragons alive. There's rarely ever more than one in existence at a time."

"Great." I groaned. There was only one king drake in the whole world, and it was crouched between Sile and me. As if the king's elite guards weren't enough. We hadn't planned to do battle with a dragon like this.

Felix nudged me with his elbow. "Look!"

Icarus was crouching down to let his rider off, and a man wearing golden armor dismounted. The Lord

General was a tall man, as tall as my father. He wore a helmet topped with a long red mane of horsehair, and a red cape that swept the ground at his heels as he moved. The Lord General walked around his enormous dragon toward where the wagon was waiting.

The elite guards driving the wagon had gotten down and unlocked the back door, and I found myself gripping the hilt of my knife again. When the door opened, the Lord General stepped in and blocked our view. I saw people getting out, and I clenched my teeth. I couldn't see who it was, and it was making me furious.

Then the Lord General stepped aside, and I saw him. Lieutenant Sile Derrick staggered in front of all four of the king's elite guards. They pushed him on, making him trip and fall. He couldn't even catch himself because his hands were still tied behind his back, so he hit the dirt face-first. They had tied a gag in his mouth and there was blood on his tunic. But he was alive.

I couldn't even be proud that I'd been right again about something happening to Sile because things were looking more hopeless than ever. We had come here to save him, to set him free, but not only were we trapped in a prison camp, but we were also facing the Lord General, his king drake, and four of the king's most accomplished private guards—not to mention all the regular prison guards who were standing watch with bows and arrows in the towers, ready to make us look like pincushions. It looked impossible.

"All right." Felix took in a deep breath and I saw his shoulders flex. "We don't have much time. I've got the gate; you follow them and when you think you've got the chance, give Beckah the signal and get Sile out of there."

I nodded, but my whole body was starting to feel numb.

"We're about to die aren't we?" he asked me suddenly, glancing back and catching me off guard with that question. He was usually so confident.

I gave a small shrug, and tried to smile. "Maybe. But remember, you were the one who wanted to see what amazing, unexpected thing I'd do next."

Felix didn't answer, but I saw his cheek turn up in a smirk as he started slinking out of our hiding place. I watched him slip from shadow to shadow, making his way carefully toward the gate.

Now it was up to me. I couldn't turn back; too much was at stake. Alone in the dark, I watched them drag Sile back to his feet and lead him deeper into the prison camp. I took a deep breath to steady myself, and balled my fists.

It was time to shake off my fear. I had to be brave. Sile was counting on me.

twenty

The elite guards were leading Sile deeper into the prison camp, pushing him whenever he stopped, and keeping a knife at his back. He wasn't fighting them as much anymore. As I crept in closer, I saw that one of his arms looked wrong. From the elbow down it was bloody, and there were pieces of white bone sticking up through the skin. Somehow, they had broken it, and I didn't want to think about how much that must have hurt.

They forced him down the stairs that led into the mining pit and disappeared. I hesitated. If I followed, I might get caught out in the open. I didn't know if there was anywhere to hide down there. I waited, looking back at the prison guards who were milling around the wagon still. They weren't looking my way. My only worry was the dragon, but with that horrible stench in the air, maybe he wouldn't smell me.

I made a dash for the nearest stairwell. As soon as I got a few steps down, I dropped into a crouch and hunkered down, trying to duck against the shadows. None of the men working below seemed to notice me. The Lord General had his back turned, saying something to Sile that I couldn't hear from so far away. All the elite guards were standing nearby, watching. But as my eyes tracked over the inside of the crater, I started to get a bad feeling.

The smell hit me like a kick to the stomach, and when I saw where it was coming from, I started to gag. The crater went down at an angle, with those dirt-carved stairwells on all sides, leading down to where the prisoners had been mining the salt out of the ground and loading those oversized wheelbarrows with it. In the very middle was a big pile of smoldering ash and debris. The embers were still burning bright red and putting off an eerie glow that made it easier to see what was going on. I didn't think much of it at first. I mean, I assumed maybe they'd just been burning trash or waste. But as my eyes adjusted to the change in light, I started noticing the white shapes in the ash.

Bones. They were bones.

There were hundreds of them, piled up like a big pyre. They had been burning the bodies of the prisoners there. The horrible stench in the air was the smell of burning flesh. As soon as I realized that, my skin got clammy and I felt like I was going to throw up.

Suddenly, I got that strange feeling that someone was watching me. Then a big hand grabbed a fistful of my hair. "What have we here?" Someone spoke over me in a rough, grumbling voice. "Out after dark, are we? Looking for a good show?"

I heard a chorus of laughs as I kicked and fought, managing to turn around and get a glimpse of the man who had me by the hair. He was a big, pear-shaped man with narrow shoulders and a belly that was being mashed into a chest plate two sizes too small. He had a trimmed beard, dark eyes, and a big scar that ran down the side of his face onto his neck. The crest on his armor was the king's eagle, but I knew he wasn't a dragonrider. Except for that crest, his armor looked like the other prison guards.

"Well, why don't we just give you a front row seat?" He grinned down at me, and his teeth were covered in yellow tobacco stains. I could just feel the evil aura coming off him like smog. He started dragging me the rest of the way down the stairs, and I fought him every step of the way. When we got close to the big pile of charred bones, I fought even harder.

The Lord General turned around to see what the commotion was. He scowled down at me, curled his lip, and sent the guard a disapproving frown. To him, I must have looked like just another prisoner here. I wasn't wearing my Fledgling's tunic and cape anymore.

"What is that, Warden?" the Lord General asked.

"A halfbreed," the man holding me by the hair chuckled. "Haven't you ever seen one before? Sneaky little rats. Some of them could about pass for human, but I can smell that elf blood in their veins a mile away. They can't fool me. And this one's decided to test my rules. Looks like he'll be meeting his ancestors sooner than scheduled!"

The Lord General just rolled his eyes, and didn't even give me a second glance as he started removing his riding gauntlets. "Do what you want, but only after the ritual is complete. I don't want you botching it. You have no idea what a chore this has been." He moved away, angrily muttering under his breath something about small favors.

When he stepped aside, I saw Sile up close for the first time since the officer's ball. He was lying on his side, his mouth bloody like someone had hit him across the face really hard. Our eyes met, and I saw something in his face I hadn't expected. Oh sure, I had expected surprise, confusion, maybe even a little anger ... but Sile looked at me with absolute terror.

He tried to speak, but his voice cracked. He just lay there, staring at me with a look that drove an ice-cold spike of panic into the center of my chest. Something was wrong. I just didn't know what it was, yet. It was as though he wanted to tell me something—something important.

The warden threw me down onto the ground only a few feet away from Sile. He put a foot on my chest to keep me from getting up, and stood there with his arms crossed. He was so big and fat I couldn't get his foot off me no matter how I tried. He smirked down at me, and ground his heel into my ribs. It hurt, but I clenched my teeth and refused to give him the satisfaction of crying out in pain.

I knew I had one choice now, just one chance. Maybe things weren't exactly going according to plan, but our plan had been pretty much ruined the moment Lyon abandoned us. I was playing this by ear, and now it was time for a diversion.

I tried to relax, to let my mind get quiet. It was easier this time, which was strange considering the last time I was in a situation like this, I'd accidentally called out a giant man-eating turtle. Something trickled down the back of my brain like a warm shiver, making my skin prickle and my whole body shudder at once. It grew more intense, until I was shivering like I was cold.

"Put it down over there," I heard the Lord General say.

I opened my eyes to see the king's elite guards carrying what looked like a big, gold-plated box. It must have been heavy, because even with four of them helping, they were still having a hard time managing it. They set it down near the smoldering pit of bones, and the Lord General stepped forward to run his hands over it thoughtfully. He stroked the intricate carvings on the lid, and a strange look of pleasure flickered across his face. He glanced up, like he was looking at someone for approval. But the only people there to look at were the elite guards, and their masked faces hid their expressions, and none of them moved an inch.

"Open it," he commanded again. "Let us begin the ritual."

My head was starting to feel uncomfortably hot. That intense shivering heat in my mind spread all over my body, and made it feel like my muscles were tingling. It definitely seemed to be coming from whatever was inside that big golden box. My heart started to pound in my ears. My body shivered, and I tried to clear my mind again.

I reached out for Mavrik with my thoughts, calling

to him just like I had before. I waited until I felt that sensation of weight in my chest to open my eyes toward the sky. "*Mavrik, it's time. Let them taste of your flame!*" I spoke in the elven language, hoping that it would still work and that none of the guards standing around me—particularly the one with his foot on my chest—would be able to understand.

The warden looked down at me with a menacing smirk. "What did you say, whelp?"

Mavrik answered him for me with a deep, bellowing roar from overhead. It was a sound I knew all too well. Everyone looked skyward, including the Lord General, who clearly hadn't been expecting any other dragons to be cruising the area.

Mavrik roared again, with Nova joining him in a chorus of fury from the air. There was an explosion of flame somewhere outside the prison camp. All the guards began to scream in alarm.

Dragon flame isn't what most people imagine. It isn't like the flames from an oven or a fireplace that stops burning once you douse them with water. Dragons spit a sticky, very acidic venom that reacts with the air and starts to burn instantly. They have two jets in the back of their throat, and can spit that potent mucus about twenty feet. It sticks to whatever it touches like milky-colored tar, and even if you manage to snuff out the flames with water, the acid will still eat away your skin in a matter of seconds. It's pretty awful stuff. Sile had once explained to me that dragons rarely spat flame unless commanded to. They used it as a defensive mechanism, to protect themselves or their eggs on the ground where they couldn't walk or run as quickly as other predators.

I smelled the pungent odor of the dragons' flame burning in my nose, and I heard men shouting, the sounds of bowstrings snapping as arrows were fired. I knew that now was my chance.

The warden wasn't looking at me. He was staring up at the sky like everyone else, looking for the dragons that were showering the ground outside the prison camp with their burning venom. I pulled out the hunting knife hidden under my tunic, and rammed it as hard as I could into his calf. Before he could react, I ripped the knife back out again. I stabbed him twice, and the warden howled in pain. He went stumbling back and finally fell over as he clutched at his bleeding leg.

I was back on my feet in an instant, rushing to where Sile lay on the ground. I cut the ropes on his hands, and pulled the gag off his mouth.

"We have to get out of here now!" I shouted over the chaos.

He was still looking at me with that weird, haunted look of terror in his eyes. I decided maybe he was just in shock. Maybe he was confused, worried he was seeing a ghost, or had been beaten to the point of being delirious.

"How … ?" he spoke in a weak voice.

"I'll explain later," I told him. "We've only got a few minutes! Hurry, you have to get up!"

A sudden rush of heat sucked all the air right out of my lungs. Something exploded on the ground only a few yards away, bursting into flame as it was showered with sticky dragon venom that caught fire immediately. It burned my eyes, and I had to shield my face. I recognized the shards of a clay jug that landed on the ground near my boots, and knew it had been Beckah. She was using the jugs of oil as explosives, keeping the guards occupied and confused while we tried to make our escape.

"It's those little fledglings from Blybrig. Don't just stand there, you fools! Shoot them!" The Lord General bellowed with fury.

At that moment, he seemed to realize who I was. He turned around slowly, leveling a burning glare on me as I was helping Sile up to his feet. I met his gaze, seeing the reflections of the flames in his eyes.

"Ah," he growled, showing me a wicked smirk. "So *you* are the little piece of halfbreed filth that has infected my ranks. I heard about you and your wild, mongrel of a drake."

I squeezed the hunting knife in my hand, putting

myself between the Lord General and Sile. "No," I said. "I'm the little piece of halfbreed filth that isn't going to let you murder my sponsor!"

"A mistake you won't live to regret, I'm afraid." His smirk broadened, and he pulled the biggest sword I'd ever seen from a sheath at his hip. It was almost as long as I was tall, made of black metal, and had the head of a dragon that looked a lot like Icarus engraved on the hilt with two red rubies for eyes.

He started to advance on me, and I got a much better appreciation for just how tall he was. My head almost came to the middle of his chest. Almost. A sense of doom loomed over my head as he started to size me up, looking over me like he was deciding which part of me he wanted to chop off first.

The dragons kept raining fire down from the sky, and I heard Icarus bellow a roar of challenge to them. Men shouted orders or screamed in pain as the acidic venom burned them. And through it all, the Lord General came striding toward me with the fires of battle reflecting off his bronze armor. Behind him, I saw the ghostly figures of the elite guards through the flames.

I braced for impact, trying to remember all my combat training. Of course, we hadn't trained for anything like this before. The Lord General outclassed me in every way possible, and I knew this was going to be my end. But if he was going to kill me, I wasn't going to let him do it without a fight—however brief it might be.

Suddenly there was another crash, another explosion of flame as Beckah threw another jug of oil. It hit that big gold-plated box, and fire belched up into the sky as it was smashed into a million pieces. The Lord General let out a primal yell of frustration, running to the remains of the box and trying to look through the wreckage like he was searching for something.

That *something* rolled across the ground toward me and came to a stop right in front of my feet.

It was some kind of orb, a big round stone the size of a grapefruit. It laid at my feet, peeking out from a charred cloth it had been wrapped in, and I could see that it was a milky, bright green color. There were strange markings on it like splotches of gold, but it didn't look like anything that had been drawn onto it by hand. The marks looked natural, like they had just formed that way somehow, but I couldn't see enough of the stone to tell if the marks made any patterns or designs.

The minute I saw it, I felt like I couldn't move. It was splattered in burning oil from the jug, and I got this eerie feeling that the stone was *looking* back at me. My whole body got cold. My hair stood on end. I felt short of breath, and suddenly that pressure in my chest became so intense that it hurt. My head started burning again.

But I couldn't look away. I was caught up in staring at the stone, feeling like I was drowning under its pale green surface.

"Don't look at it!" Sile was right behind me. He smacked his only working hand over my eyes and started pulling me away.

Immediately, I snapped out of my trance.

He was right. This is the chance we'd been hoping for.

Together, Sile and I ran for the front gate. We dodged screaming prisoners who were running from their burning shacks, guards trying to put out the fires, and falling jugs that exploded into new bursts of flame. Sile was hurt badly. He had a hard time running, but he couldn't exactly lean on me since I was half his size. He staggered and stumbled, and a few times I had to use all my strength to keep him from falling.

Finally, I saw the gate. It was cracked open already, and Felix was standing just outside it with his eyes wide in horror at the chaos we'd unleashed. I saw him looking through the blazing madness, desperately searching for us. When he spotted us struggling to get away from the chaos, he didn't hesitate for a single second. He sprinted toward us and put Sile's good arm around his shoulder, helping him along as we made our final dash for the open prison camp gate.

As we ran out of the prison gate, my spirits soared with new hope. We had made it out. Sile was with us. We had rescued him. And I thought for an instant that it was over. I thought we were free.

I was wrong.

When we stopped to catch our breath, waiting for Beckah to descend with Mavrik and Nova and carry us away into the night, I made the mistake of looking back. From back inside the prison camp, I heard a deafening roar that shook the ground under my feet. Dragon flame burst through the prison camp gate, melting the iron and turning it to a pile of molten mush in a matter of seconds.

Icarus came crawling out of the inferno like a demon straight out of the pits of hell. His red eyes gleamed, and the flames danced over his glossy black scales. He hissed, baring rows of dripping fangs as he charged straight for us, ready to burn us all to ash. On his back, I could see the Lord General sitting in the saddle with his sword still drawn. I could have sworn I heard him laughing over the roaring of his dragon and the rush of the flames.

Icarus was coming for us, and there was no way we could outrun him. Huddled together, looking into the fires of doom, Felix, Sile, and I exchanged a meaningful look. This was it. We were trapped like rats, with nothing to cling to now except each other.

I closed my eyes again for a moment, and then looked

up to the sky. Finding that quiet place in my mind was easy for some reason, even in the face of certain death. The sound of Icarus growling became distant, and my thoughts were crystal clear.

"Don't come down here, Mavrik." I told him. I knew he would hear, and he'd be furious that I was refusing his help again. "We can't let Beckah get hurt. If you bring her down here, she would be killed with the rest of us. I can't let that happen, so don't land. It's all right."

Then something strange happened, something that had never happened before.

Mavrik answered me.

It wasn't with words. I saw a flash of images in my mind, like a dream only I wasn't sleeping. Mavrik was sending me these images, communicating with me through pictures and colors. First he showed me a flash of our first encounter, when I'd made my deal with him. Then he showed me the giant paludix turtle that I'd called out of the marsh. Finally, I saw myself standing in front of Icarus, while the huge king drake lowered his head in submission.

Suddenly, I knew what I had to do. Mavrik had given me the answer. I stood up, pushing away from the others and beginning to walk toward Icarus.

Felix shouted after me, "What are you doing?!"

I didn't look back at him. "I'm going to have a word

with the king."

Icarus came to a halt directly in front of me. He towered so far above me that he blended into the night sky, and all I could see of his head were his two glowing red eyes. He snarled, his lips curling back to show me rows of jagged teeth that were dripping with that burning venom.

"Crush his bones," the Lord General commanded. "Leave nothing but ash for his friends to bury."

Icarus hissed and seemed happy to oblige. He started to lower his massive spine-covered head down toward me. I could hear him taking in a breath, preparing to blast me with a spray of his flame.

I knew what I had to do. Icarus was a king drake, the most powerful of his kind. Sile had told me before that once dragons chose their riders, that they shared a bond of comradery, but now they were treated more like livestock. That was why my connection with Mavrik was so special; he had chosen me and accepted me as his rider of his own free will. But chances were, that hadn't been the case for Icarus. Now, I was about to put that to the ultimate test.

"Great king, please hear me," I called out to Icarus. I went down onto one knee before the king drake, showing him reverence he'd probably never been given before. "Why are you taking orders from a rider you didn't choose? He's ordering you to kill me, but I come to you with respect and ask you to show me mercy. Remember who you are. Don't let this human rule you. You owe him nothing!"

Icarus paused. His bottomless red eyes were staring right at me, boring into my soul. I could sense how powerful he was, how wise and old. And now he was listening to me.

"What right does he have to command you?" I continued. "A king should have the right to choose who rides upon his back. No one should force that choice upon you, or any of your kin! Take back your freedom!"

The king drake growled. I saw his big nostrils puff, sampling my scent with a deep breath that made my hair blow wildly around my head.

"What are you doing?!" The Lord General screamed with rage. "You stupid beast, do as you're told! Burn him until his bones are nothing but charred coals!"

All of a sudden, Icarus turned on him. He spread his leather black wings, reared back onto his hind legs, and let out another booming roar. But this time, it wasn't directed at me.

As I started to run back toward Sile and Felix, I saw the king drake whip his head around and strip the saddle off his back with his teeth, taking the Lord General with it. I heard the sound of screaming, pleading, and dragon teeth against armor. I couldn't bear to watch Icarus devour his own rider, so I just ducked my head and kept running.

Felix and Sile were already hobbling away as fast as they could. When I caught up to them, I tried to help Felix carry Sile's weight. We made it away from the burning prison camp safely to the rolling grassy hills of the farmland beyond. By then, the dragonriders from the castle were circling over head, looking for what had caused this mess, but Mavrik and Nova were already long gone. Soldiers and people from the city were trying to put out the blaze.

I, for one, wasn't sad at all to see that horrible place go up in smoke.

We laid Sile down in the grass, and sat down to catch our breath. We didn't speak at first. Instead, we just sat there watching the prison camp burn against the night sky.

Sile grabbed my arm and squeezed it tightly, looking up at me with a sense of urgency. "Never do that again," he growled.

"Call to a dragon?" I wasn't sure what he meant. I'd done a lot of things recently I probably shouldn't have.

"No," he said hoarsely, and his grip on my arm weakened a little. "Risk your life for mine."

twenty-one

Beckah was waiting for us at the corner of the same farmer's field where we had stolen the tools. She was standing between Mavrik and Nova with the night wind blowing in her long dark hair. When she saw us coming, her eyes filled with tears, and she ran toward us with her arms open wide.

Beckah hugged her father tightly, and he put his good arm around her while he kissed the top of her head. "Beck!" His voice quavered, and I saw tears in his eyes as well. "What are you doing here?"

It was a long story, and there wasn't time right then to go hash it all out for him. It would just have to wait. We had to get as far away from that prison camp as possible.

Sile saddled up with Felix, Beckah sat with me, and we took off into the twilight and left the prison camp far behind.

As she sat in front of me, I saw Beckah smiling again. It made my stomach swim with nervousness. She took my arm and wrapped it around her waist so she could squeeze it tightly, and my insides just squirmed harder.

"Thank you so much, Jae," she said, looking back at me over her shoulder. "You're amazing." She was sitting so close to me that her nose almost touched mine when she turned back to see me. I could count every freckle on her cheeks and nose.

I blushed so hard I could barely see straight. "You're welcome." I didn't know what else to say.

Over on Nova's back, I caught a glimpse of Sile staring at us. He didn't look very happy. In fact, I could have sworn he was glaring daggers at me. I quickly leaned back away from Beckah, and took my arm out from around her waist.

It was a long trip back to Blybrig. We flew all the way without stopping, finally landing outside the breaking dome as the sun began to set. There was a big group of instructors and students waiting there for us as soon as we touched down. I noticed that there were also armored city guards from Halfax standing around, men the king must have sent. I recognized the style of their armor from when I lived with my mother in the ghetto. That made dread hit me like a kick to the gut.

The other instructors were quick to help us get Sile down out of the saddle. They carried him toward the infirmary, because he was so weak. As he disappeared through the crowd, Beckah followed closely behind and held on to his good hand. Felix and I were left standing there awkwardly by our dragons, wondering what would happen to us now.

Everyone was staring right at us. Students, instructors, even the guards were just standing there with expressions I couldn't interpret. No one said a word.

Felix and I looked horrible. We were both still wearing the tunics Felix had cut out of old grain sacks, and we were caked with smelly mud from the marsh. We were filthy, hungry, and completely exhausted. But no one was looking at us with pity or sympathy. No one seemed glad to see us, either. I couldn't help but wonder if we were about to be kicked out of Blybrig, or arrested. I didn't even want to think about how many rules we had broken.

Finally, the somber-faced instructor standing nearest to me went down onto one knee, putting a fist on the ground as he bowed to us. Like a ripple, all the others in the crowd began to do the same—even the guards from Halfax. Felix and I exchanged a wide-eyed glance. I couldn't believe what I was seeing. I was pretty certain no one had ever bowed to a halfbreed like this before.

No one tried to stop us when we finally went to put our dragons away in the Roost. I took my time removing Mavrik's saddles and feeding him big hunks of raw meat. I ran my hands over his scaly head, scratching him behind the ears until I heard him begin to purr. He looked at me with his bright yellow eyes. I got an eerie feeling when I remembered how he'd spoken back to me at the prison camp. He really did understand it when I talked to him, and he now could communicate back.

"Thank you," I said as I rubbed his snout. "I'm lucky to have you as a partner."

Mavrik made a happy chirping noise, and the image of us flying together flashed through my mind. It startled me. I couldn't stop grinning at him. "Get some rest. I'd say we've both earned it."

He didn't waste any time. He bedded down in his nest of straw, putting his nose on his tail and closing his eyes. I could still hear him purring to himself as I left his stall and went back down the stairs.

I knew that sooner or later, Felix and I were going to have to answer for what we'd done. It wasn't like no one had noticed we were missing. But thankfully, training had been suspended until we were found. And now that we were back, Academy Commander Rayken gave everyone a few days to settle down before training resumed. It gave me time to eat and sleep as much as I wanted.

Three days later, early in the morning, Felix and I got the order that Commander Rayken wanted to see us immediately. Felix looked nervous, but I had already come to terms with the fact that this was probably the end of my career as a dragonrider. I was going to take all the blame, since it had been all my idea in the first place, and Commander Rayken was going to formally dismiss me from Blybrig. At least, that's what I was expecting.

Dressed in clean fledgling uniforms, we walked together to his office without saying a word. We didn't look at each other as we climbed the stairs and waited outside the door. Felix knocked, and I heard Commander Rayken's voice telling us to come inside.

We stood side-by-side at attention in front of his desk with our hands clasped behind our backs. I didn't dare meet his eyes as Commander Rayken looked us over with a steely expression. It was hard to tell what kind of mood he was in, since I had only seen him a few times before, and he apparently never smiled. He had hard lines on his face from his constant frown, and something about his features reminded me of an old cranky owl.

"You two have made my life very complicated, as of late," he said at last. "First with the saddle nonsense, and now this."

"Sir," Felix spoke up suddenly. "Permission to speak freely?"

The Commander narrowed his eyes and nodded.

"This was my fault, sir. I take sole responsibility for what happened." He squared his shoulders, looking like he was having a hard time holding himself together.

At first, all I could do was stare at him. I didn't even realize my mouth was hanging open until a few minutes had gone by. "B-but that's not—"

Felix shot me an angry look. "It was, Jae. I could have stopped you from leaving Brinton's estate, but I didn't. I'm the oldest, so I'm responsible."

"It's admirable to try and spare him from punishment," the Commander interrupted us suddenly. "But I'm afraid your friend came to me personally in the ballroom asking for my help. You were nowhere in sight, Mr. Farrow."

Felix's face flushed, and he glared down at the tops of his boots. He didn't say anything else.

Commander Rayken's gaze turned on me then, and I found myself wrenching my sweaty hands together behind my back. "Do you remember when you first came here?" he asked me. "Lieutenant Derrick was adamant that I should allow you to join our brotherhood. He insisted that having you here would help restore our fading legacy of honor and discipline."

I tensed, waiting for the axe to drop. As ready as I'd

thought I was before to hear him kick me out of Blybrig, I was so nervous I was shaking. I didn't want my time as a dragonrider to be over.

Commander Rayken sighed as he leaned forward to rest his elbows on his desk. "As much as it pains me to admit it—he was right."

I was stunned. For the second time, I couldn't speak. All I could do was stand there, staring at him with my mouth hanging open again.

"You have demonstrated courage that only befits a dragonrider," he went on. "Apparently, in saving your sponsor, you also prevented the success of a plot to defile a sacred artifact that would have granted the Lord General immortality. That power hungry fool stole from the king, paid off some of the royal elite guards to join his cause, and infiltrated my academy. He betrayed his own brothers, whom he had sworn to protect and lead as Lord General, in the most profound way imaginable. It's only fitting that his own dragon went mad and devoured him. Good riddance."

Felix and I exchanged a meaningful glance. We both knew Icarus hadn't really gone mad. I had been the one encouraging the king drake to rebel, although eating the Lord General was entirely the dragon's idea.

"You're talking about the god stone?" I dared to ask.

The Commander just sighed again, fidgeting with

papers on his desk. "Yes. Some call it the god stone. The king prizes it as the crown jewel of his reign. It's all magical nonsense, really. It's ridiculous, thinking a rock could grant anyone immortal life."

I felt a little queasy when I thought about the stone I'd seen through the flames in the prison camp. That milky green orb wrapped in a cloth had lain right at my feet. It entranced me somehow, as though it had some sort of force to pull me in. Remembering it gave me chills.

"But why did he want to kill Sile?" I murmured under my breath. I recalled that the Lord General had said something about a ritual that needed to be performed. "What did Sile have to do with a ritual like that?"

"Why don't you ask him yourself?" Commander Rayken grumbled. "He's leaving this afternoon. The infirmary has declared him physically unfit for duty. He's being medically discharged as of today. From now on, you will both be sponsored by Lieutenant Rordin."

It took a moment for that to sink in. Sile wasn't coming back. He wouldn't be my sponsor anymore. The minute I got that news, it felt like my career was doomed. Sile had looked out for me and been forgiving to my small size and pathetic strength. He'd never cared that I was a halfbreed. I didn't know who Lieutenant Rordin was, but I seriously doubted he was going to approve of me.

I looked at Felix, wondering if he'd known about this already. Judging by the total shock I saw on his face, clearly he hadn't.

"Training will formally resume tomorrow, so I suggest you both prepare," Commander Rayken said, wafting his hand at us as though he were shooing us away. "You are dismissed."

As soon as we got back outside, Felix turned to me with a sly grin. He grabbed my shoulders with excitement, and started shaking me like a rag doll. "Can you believe that?! Do you have any idea how lucky we are? I thought for sure we were both about to get the boot!"

I smirked back at him. "So did I, but we should probably go talk to Sile."

His smile faded a little, and he let me go. "Yeah. He's bound to be pretty upset about getting medically discharged."

To be honest, the idea of seeing Sile again made me nervous. I didn't know what would be left of the man I'd looked up to like, well, like the father I'd never really had. Sile had always been so dignified and proud, a true dragonrider in my mind. Seeing him battered, broken, and now officially dismissed from service was going to be difficult.

We made our way to the infirmary building as the sun was beginning to dip below the mountains. When we arrived, a medic in a white tunic told us to wait in the foyer while he asked if Sile was willing to have visitors. I'd never been in the infirmary before, but it had a very pungent odor from all the medicines. When the medic returned, he told us to follow him and showed us the way up a flight of stairs to the second floor. There were lots of rooms for patients, but most of them were empty with only a single clean, white bed inside.

Sile was sitting on the edge of his bed with his whole left arm wrapped layer upon layer of gauze. I could see that his forearm was splinted, and only the tips of his fingers peeked out of the dressings. His lip was still swollen, he had a nasty bruise on his jaw and around one of his eyes, but he still managed to look like the proud warrior he was.

He was talking to Beckah in a soft voice where she sat in a chair near the doorway. When we came in, they both looked up. Beckah's face brightened as she smiled at me. She stood up and threw her arms around my waist, hugging me tightly, and then doing the same thing to Felix. Sile didn't seem to approve of that, even though he didn't say anything to stop her. I could see his expression stiffen into a tense frown.

"Beck?" He cleared his throat to get her attention. "Why don't you go see about getting us some dinner before we get on the road back home? I could use a bite to eat."

She beamed at him before she went skipping out of the room, her long dark braid trailing behind her. Our eyes met as she passed, and she winked at me playfully. It made me smirk a little and blush again in spite of myself.

When I looked back at Sile, he was glaring at me like he wanted to hit me. "Would anyone care to explain to me why you took my little girl on your suicidal rescue attempt?"

I was getting the feeling he expected *me* to answer that. I opened my mouth to come up with some kind of excuse, but Felix beat me to it. "She insisted on coming," he said. "She refused to let us leave her behind."

Sile cut him a murderous look. "She is a fourteen year old child. You're nearly a man. Surely you can see how I have a hard time believing she forced you to do anything."

I swallowed hard. "Sir, we were afraid whoever kidnapped you might take her, too."

"She could have been killed," he snapped. I heard him sigh as he started rubbing his forehead with his good hand. "You all could have been killed, and that would be on my head. I would be standing before my ancestors with the blood of three children on my hands in addition to … " His voice trailed away, and he just sat there staring vacantly ahead of him.

"Sir?" I started to ask. There were so many things I

wanted to know that I really didn't know where to start. "Why you? If the Lord General needed some kind of a sacrifice for the ritual to grant him immortality, why did he pick you? Couldn't he have just picked an easier victim?"

Sile met my gaze again, and this time he looked confused. "Immortality? Is that what they're saying?"

Felix and I both nodded.

He chuckled hoarsely like that was ridiculous, shaking his head. "Lies," he muttered. "Lies, as usual."

"Sir?" I was anxious for him to explain.

Sile just kept shaking his head while he ran his fingers over the thick bandaging on his arm. "In this case, knowing too much can most certainly kill you. Let what happened to me be an example for you of what happens when you know too much. What I know has almost taken my life twice. It's better that you know nothing, for now."

I didn't like that answer, and judging by the sour look on Felix's face, neither did he. We'd been through a lot just to be shut down without any idea what was going on with Sile. I felt like he owed us something more than that vague explanation. "But what if they come for you again? If we don't know what we're up against—"

"They won't," he interrupted. "I'm not a threat to them anymore. The medics have said that my arm will heal, but I have lost almost all sensation in my hand. I cannot grip a fork with out great effort, much less a sword or a dragon saddle. I am useless in the eyes of the king now. Valla will be released to join the other dragons in the wild, and I will go home to my family in retirement."

Sile didn't sound happy about that at all. His expression was somber as he stared at the floor, and I could see the look of distress in his eyes. I couldn't imagine how lost he must have felt, suddenly having his life's career ripped out from underneath him. Even so, when he sighed, I caught his eyes for just a brief second. It made me wonder if he really was telling us the truth. Was he really safe now?

"And we're being passed on to someone else. Lieutenant Rordin—whoever that is," Felix grumbled.

"Jace Rordin is a good man," Sile said. "I fought alongside him when I was a younger man. He's only just now retired from the front lines. If you're smart, you'll listen to what he has to say. He'll have valuable information and tactics to share with you that most riders don't have, because of his experience."

He paused then, looking over at me as though he could sense what I was wondering: Had Sile told him that I was a halfbreed? He smirked and gave a small shrug. "I told him you were unique, but you are the bravest fledgling I'd ever met. Brave to the point of suicidal, in fact."

Hearing that made me deflate. "I wasn't brave. I was terrified the whole time."

Sile gave me a strange look then, as though what I said disappointed him. "Bravery is not an immunity to fear, it is rising up to meet it with the hope that nothing is impossible."

I shifted uneasily where I stood as Sile just sat there staring at us. After a few uncomfortable moments, Beckah came back in carrying two plates piled with food. She glanced at all of us as she put the plates down on the bedside table. I could tell she was trying to figure out what was wrong. Finally, she looked at her father with a worried expression.

Sile just smiled at her. "Maybe you'd like to go eat with them in the dining hall, instead?"

Her face lit up suddenly, and she looked back at us hopefully. "Daddy, are you sure? I already brought something up here."

He just waved a hand at her dismissively, "I can eat both. I haven't had anything in days. I'll be fine. Go on."

I had a feeling he just wanted to get rid of us for a while. Despite the way he smiled at her, I could still see sadness in his dark eyes. This was hard for him; it just had to be. Leaving Blybrig meant his days as a dragonrider were over forever, and I could imagine how that would terrify someone who had been doing this since he was our age.

"I'll come by next year and see how you two are progressing," Sile called after us on our way out the door. "So don't disappoint me."

I swore right then that I would do my best not to. Out of every other dragonrider here, his opinion was the one I valued the most. I wanted his approval more than anyone else's. I wanted to make him proud of me.

twenty-two

Two days later, Lyon was back, and standing in formation at the call to arms. He looked pretty horrible—like he hadn't slept since he'd abandoned us at the prison camp. There were dark circles under his eyes, and he wouldn't tell anyone what had happened or where he'd been. It took me a while to talk Felix down from wanting to beat the life out of him right then and there. I thought I'd succeeded, but then I spotted Lyon in the dormitory hallway later that night and he had a fresh black eye. I didn't have to wonder who'd given it to him.

I was relieved when training started up again. It was comforting to be back where everything made sense, and all my days were planned down to the last minute.

I had a warm bed, three good meals, and I got to train with Mavrik every day. I didn't tell anyone about my new ability to communicate with him, or that he could speak back to me by sending me images in my mind. Considering how most people were responding to me calling to animals, I decided it was probably best to keep that to myself, for now.

Felix and I got back into our old routines like nothing had ever happened, well … except for our new sponsor. Lieutenant Jace Rordin was a lot different than Sile. When he met us for the first time, I got the impression right away that he wasn't going to put up with any nonsense. He looked like he was in his mid thirties, but I would have never thought of him as old. He was a fairly normal height, with an average build, dark eyes under a serious brow, and dark brown hair that was beginning to turn gray along his sideburns and temples. He had a grim, somber look about him just like you would expect from a man who'd just returned from the battlefront.

When he looked at me, it made my shoulders seize up instinctively because I was always afraid of what he'd say to me. He'd just gotten finished killing gray elves, and I knew what I looked like. But he never said a word about my heritage, which only made me more anxious.

Jace may not have looked like anyone extraordinary, but he was a very good swordfighter. He kept us doing the same drills every the morning Sile had started with us, only … he made us get up even earlier and actually did them with us. He even ran laps with us. Then he started teaching us more about sparring and hand-to-had combat techniques, advanced stuff that the other fledglings weren't learning yet.

He pushed us to our breaking point every single day. I could tell that my size and lack of strength were annoying to him. He was constantly critiquing me, insisting that I needed to work harder, and shaking his head like I was a big disappointment.

I still wasn't any good with the weaponry we were learning to use. Swords were still too big and heavy, and I could barely pull back a bowstring. It was frustrating, but I muscled through. I wasn't going to give up. If Rordin was trying to break me by proving I wasn't strong enough to stay here, then he'd just have to toss my body out on the doorstep after I died from doing too many pushups.

"You need to keep up this regimen during the interlude," Jace growled at my heels as he ran behind us during morning laps. "Every day you should run, fly drills, and work on building your strength and stamina."

I didn't know what the interlude was. It seemed to be a pretty big deal though, because the whole academy started buzzing about it as training went on. Instructors looked more serious and pushed us even harder. The avian class ahead of us started to look more stressed and worried. You could practically taste the tension in the air.

On our last week of training before the interlude, Felix explained that while training for the older students went year-round, fledglings got a three month break while the class ahead of us, the avians, learned ground survival techniques. It all focused around that final month where all the avian students were put through a rigorous final test they called the battle scenario.

"That'll be us next year, you know. It's the most intense training we'll ever do," he said. "They teach us how to endure interrogation, torture, and how to survive in Luntharda if we get shot down behind enemy lines. Students have died during this training. It's no joke. All the instructors have to be present to help out."

Now I was starting to understand why Jace was pushing me so hard. If that training was difficult, or even deadly, to normal students … I could only imagine what it was going to be like for me. Jace must have been concerned that I was too small to survive, and I couldn't really blame him for that.

"We won't have our dragons to help us. They'll have some kind of goal for us, usually it's to evade capture as long as possible, and you have to survive being eaten by monsters or starving to death. Then once everyone's been caught, the instructor's start the mock interrogation."

"Mock interrogation?" I didn't like the sound of that.

Felix just shrugged. "Yeah, but we'll get specialized training on how to handle it. It'll be fine."

I wasn't so sure. Well, I knew Felix would probably be all right. He was strong and probably one of the best hand-to-hand fighters in our class. My own skill set was still questionable, though. I wasn't sure talking to animals would do me any good.

When training finally began to wind down, the other fledglings made preparations to go back home for our three-month break. Felix was going back to his parents' estate. He kept asking me over and over if I wanted to stay with him and train. He insisted his parents wouldn't mind, or that they probably wouldn't even notice I was there at all.

"They barely notice me and I'm their only child." He chuckled as he packed his clothes and uniforms back into his bags.

"It sounds great," I said. "It's not because I don't want to. There's just, well, there's someone I need to see."

He turned a sly grin in my direction. "Your girl, huh?"

I blushed. "I told you, it's not like that. But I promised her I'd see her as soon as I could."

He kept grinning as he went back to packing. "Sure, sure. You've got quite a tale to tell her, huh? You think she'll believe any of it?"

"I don't know. I guess it is kind of a wild story." I rubbed my thumb over my mother's necklace, toying with it while I sat on the edge of my bed. I'd already packed all of my things up, but I didn't want to leave until I absolutely had to.

Going back home was bittersweet. On the one hand, I was excited to see Katty again and tell her about everything. But then there was my family. I wasn't looking forward to seeing them again, and being forced to sleep in the loft, or blamed for everything by my stepmother and her two little demon daughters. I knew being a dragonrider wasn't going to change anything when it came to them.

Felix finished packing and picked up his bags, nodding for me to follow him as we left our room behind. We walked together one last time down the stairs, out of the dormitory, and across the open grounds toward the Roost. I took my time putting Mavrik's saddle on. Out of the corner of my eye, I could see that Felix was doing the same. Neither of us wanted to leave, I guess.

When we met back outside the Roost, it was awkward. I didn't want to admit it to him, but I was going to miss Felix. He'd become my best friend to replace Katty when she wasn't around. Not having him there to watch my back, or tease me about my love life, was going to make it hard to get through three months of dealing with my family.

"Well, if you need anything, send me a letter. Or just show up, if you want." He was looking at me with a worried expression. "Hey, uh … you're a dragonrider now. So don't let anyone push you around. You don't have to put up with that anymore."

I smiled at him. "I'll try to remember that."

"And keep training, like Lieutenant Rordin said," he added. "Next year will be twice as hard as this one. You need to be ready."

"Right."

"And, seriously, if you want to come visit for a few days—"

"Felix?"

He paused. "Yeah?"

I smirked, reared back, and gave him a punch in the arm as hard as I could. "I'll be fine. See you in three months."

He just rolled his eyes because my punch didn't even make him flinch. "Says the kid with noodles for arms," he mumbled under his breath. Finally, he just gave me one of his sly, crooked smiles and gave me a swat on the back of the head.

I stood there for a few moments and watched him walk away. He climbed up onto Nova's back, fastening down his luggage before he gave me one last wave and took off into the sky. I watched them go, climbing higher and higher, until they were nothing more than a tiny dark speck on the horizon.

Mavrik lowered his head and started making those curious chirping sounds and blinking his big yellow eyes at me. A crystal-clear image of Felix and I playing chase through the sky on the backs of our dragons flashed through my mind. I knew it came from Mavrik.

I turned around to pat his snout. "Yeah," I told him. "Don't worry. We'll see them again."

THE END

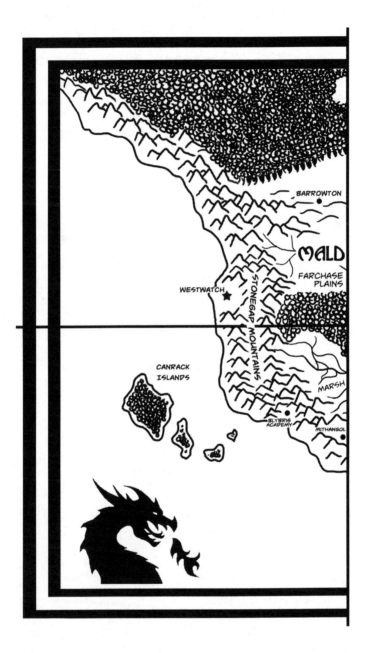

BARROWTON

MALD

FARCHASE
PLAINS

WESTWATCH

STONEGAP MOUNTAINS

CANRACK
ISLANDS

MARSH

BLYBRIS
ACADEMY

MITHANGOL

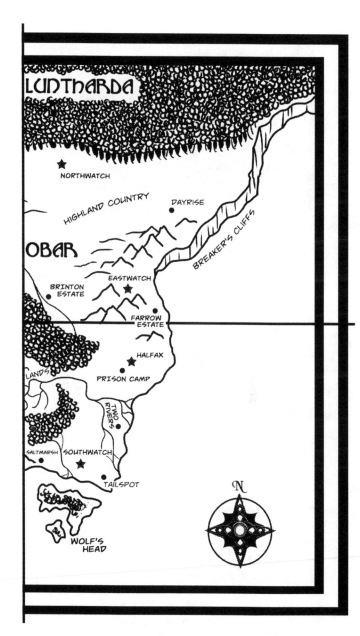

Nicole Conway

Nicole is the author of the children's fantasy series, THE DRAGONRIDER CHRONICLES, about a young boy's journey into manhood as he trains to become a dragonrider. She has completed the first two books in the series, and is now working on the third and final book.

Originally from a small town in North Alabama, Nicole moves frequently due to her husband's career as a pilot for the United States Air Force. She received a B.A. in English with a concentration in Classics from Auburn University, and will soon attend graduate school.

She has previously worked as a freelance and graphic artist for promotional companies, but has now embraced writing as a full-time occupation.

Nicole enjoys hiking, camping, shopping, cooking, and spending time with her family and friends. She also loves watching children's movies and collecting books. She lives at home with her husband, two cats, and a dog.

OTHER MONTH9BOOKS TITLES YOU MIGHT
LIKE

AVIAN
TRAITOR
THE THREE THORNS

Find more awesome Teen books at http://www.
Month9Books.com

Connect with Month9Books online:
Facebook: www.Facebook.com/Month9Books
Twitter: https://twitter.com/Month9Books
You Tube: www.youtube.com/user/Month9Books
Blog: www.month9booksblog.com
Instagram: https://instagram.com/month9books
Request review copies via publicity@month9books.com

Avian

NICOLE CONWAY

Traitor

NICOLE CONWAY

THE
BROTHERHOOD
AND THE
SHIELD
THE THREE THORNS

MICHAEL GIBNEY